Faithful Valor

Faithful Valor

Isabella

SAPPHIRE BOOKS

SALINAS, CALIFORNIA

Editor - Heather Flournoy
Book Design - LJ Reynolds
Cover Design - Fineline Cover Design

Sapphire Books Publishing, LLC
P.O. Box 8142
Salinas, CA 93912
www.sapphirebooks.com

Printed in the United States of America
First Edition – December 2019

This and other Sapphire Books titles can be found at
www.sapphirebooks.com

Dedication

For Schileen, always for Schileen.

This book is dedicated to all who serve and suffer in silence. You are my heros.

Acknowledgments

It takes a team to get a book ready to go to publication. Thank you to my editor, Heather Flournoy. She is always amazing and knows just what I mean, even when I don't.

To the copy editors and proofers. They make me slap our heads and say, duh.

LJ Reynolds, your hard work is amazing.

To the readers. Thank you for ten years. You make it all worth it.

Isabella

Prologue

Smells of gasoline, oil, and rubber permeated the air that swirled around Nic Caldwell. Flecks of dust danced in the diffused light streaming over her shoulder. She stood and stretched her back, then leaned against the workbench as she studied her motorcycle. It needed a good polish, the kind that took hours of concentration, silence, a toothbrush, and copious amounts of rubbing compound. The chrome had pitted in a few places, but nothing she couldn't work out.

The sound of children's laughter floated in the breeze on the other side of the garage door. A palm slapping a rubber ball against the cement of the driveway echoed in the garage. Nic smiled, recognizing Grace's giggle and then little Timmy's voice beckoning her to try and hit him with the ball.

On one side of the steel barrier, life was going on as usual. Nic rolled the mechanic's stool closer to her motorcycle and rubbed the compound on a spot on the chrome. Circling her fingers wider, the swirl of chrome polish took on a haze as it started to dry. Snapping the red shop rag, she stuffed it into her back pocket, picked up the toothbrush, and caked on more compound and worked it into the fins of the engine. Detail work like this kept her focused and her mind busy. She told Claire it was her Zen time. More specifically, it was her way of escaping the outside world, hidden in her garage, away from the reality of day-to-day existence.

Nic grasped the worn knot on the end of the gnarled cane. Her palm slid smoothly into place before she pushed off the bench. Putting her weight on the stick, she hobbled over to her motorcycle. She'd tried to straddle it a couple of weeks ago, but her hip had protested too loudly. She shielded her eyes from the afternoon sun as it pushed farther into the garage. The sunlight gave her a piercing headache without her sunglasses. Was it the temporary side effect of her ocular nerve being pinched, or was it the concussion? She couldn't remember. Hell, she was lucky to be able to see at all. Rubbing her temple, her fingertips ran along the hairline scar from her operation. Lately she was feeling more like a troll that lived under a bridge, only venturing out when it was dark, her signature hoodie pulled over her face when she went jogging. Her routine had morphed into late nights and hours and hours spent in the garage. Slowly, she was trying to force herself to get back into a schedule that would mesh with her family's life.

Swirls. Lots of swirls covered the tank as she lost herself in the work of polishing.

Silence. The glorious sound of nothingness. Pushing back the stool, she admired the symmetry of the lines of polish covering her bike.

Bang. Bang. Bang.

Nic flew to the floor as screams erupted around her. She tucked her head to her chest and covered it with her hands, her knees drawn up as close as she could bring them.

Nic glanced around her, but she couldn't see anything in the pitch black. It was surreal. One minute she's hearing Grace outside, the next she's standing alone. Her body felt like it was on fire, coupled with the distinct smell of something burning. Nic turned to her right. The sergeant standing next to her was on fire.

"Sergeant, you're burning."

"Ma'am?"

"Sergeant, look." Nic pointed to the sergeant's arms. "Fire."

Blackness again.

"Nic, honey?" Claire stood over Nic, smiling down at her.

"What are you doing here, baby?" Nic touched Claire's face. Her bloody fingers left a trail down the delicate pink skin of Claire's neck. Turning her hands over, Nic saw the skin was broken, bleeding, and charred. The coppery smell assaulted her as she tried to wipe the blood off Claire's face. "I'm sorry, sweetheart." The smudges only grew as she pushed her broken fingers across Claire's skin and down her white dress.

A piercing scream sliced the air. Nic covered her mouth, her throat tight.

Something slammed against the garage door again, paralyzing Nic. Her body was frozen in place as she tried to take a deep breath. Her chest was so tight she could barely force air in, let alone out. She heard more screaming, and then laughing.

A door slammed somewhere in the background.

"Nic. Nic, are you okay?" Claire scooped Nic up into her arms and began rocking her. "I'm so sorry, sweetheart. I should have told Grace to stop with the ball and I didn't get outside in time."

Nic lay cradled, unable to move, in Claire's arms. Pain lanced through her head. She squeezed her eyes tight, blocking out the light in hopes that it would ease the sharpness. She buried herself in Claire's embrace, hoping the touch of her lover would ease her suffering.

It didn't.

Another bang against the door and Nic's body began to shake uncontrollably.

"Oh, sweetheart. Let's get you in the house."

Claire struggled to lift Nic. Nic's body was jelly as she struggled to push off the floor. Her brain was a fog bank and offered little help complying as the pain pierced through her head with every movement. Getting to her knees, she stopped Claire. She had a sudden urge to throw up. Her throat constricted. Swallowing hard, she rocked back and forth.

"Give me a second." She gripped Claire's forearms to steady herself.

"Take your time, sweetheart."

Nic shielded her eyes from the light streaming in. She'd had migraines before, but this was a headache on steroids. Her doctor had warned her that they could last for hours, or days. There was no rhyme or reason for the sudden onset, but Nic had noticed that when her PTSD raged, so did the pain in her head. The loud bang of the ball against the door was just the type of trigger she tried to avoid, but life was full of triggers. She'd have to learn to cope with them if she wanted to move forward in her career and not be a hermit.

Pushing herself to standing, she wavered. Claire wrapped Nic's arm around her shoulder and hefted Nic up. Nic couldn't help but notice the unsubtle symbolism of Claire being her rock now, quite literally holding her up and helping her. She'd abdicated her role as the head of the family, but not willingly. She struggled with the idea that she wasn't in a position to take care of her family. This was just another example of the abdication.

"Come on, sweetheart." Claire guided Nic toward the door, each step a struggle.

"I'm sorry, honey."

"I'm the one that should be sorry. I was so busy in the house I didn't even think about the kids playing outside."

"We can't keep that little peanut cooped up in the house. She needs to be outside playing and being a kid." Nic closed her eyes, trying to ease the pain. "It's not her fault. Don't say anything to her, please."

"I should probably just keep her busy with quiet playtime."

"Seriously, honey. There is no such thing as a quiet game if kids get rowdy, and they always do. It's part of growing up. Relax, I'll be fine. I just need to lie down for a while."

Her bedroom was dark, cool, and inviting. Claire gently set Nic on the bed, bent down and started to take off her boots. Nic lay back and let Claire undress her down to her underwear. If she wasn't struggling so badly, she'd reach up and pull her lover down on top of her and ravish her. Unfortunately, her head had other plans.

"Here, sweetheart. Take these." Claire handed Nic the migraine meds the doctor had prescribed. They worked better if she took them at the onset, but this one had jumped on her like a wicked ex-lover with revenge on her mind.

"Thanks." Pain cut through her head as she cocked it back to swallow her meds. "Fuck."

"Oh, babe. Can I get you anything else? Maybe a cold cloth for your head, ice, anything?"

Truth be told, she just wanted quiet, but she wouldn't tell Claire. "I think I'll just try and sleep. Do you mind?"

Claire kissed her forehead. "I'll try and keep the kids quiet."

"Thanks."

Nic wanted to cry. Lately she'd had more days like today than fewer. At least her physical injuries and ailments were visible and could be treated, however minimally. Mentally, on the other hand, she wasn't as far along as she'd hoped despite great strides made in the treatment of PTSD. She didn't want to become a statistic. She'd heard too many stories of servicemembers who couldn't deal with the pain they brought home and took the only way out they could see.

Suicide.

She had to remind herself often that she had a family, career, and life that she wanted to hang on to for as long as possible. However, sometimes it was hard to focus on the long term and not look for relief in the bottom of a bottle of pills or alcohol…or worse.

⁂

Claire rounded up the kids and walked down the street to Timmy's house. His mom was outside spraying the freshly planted flowers. She waved at Claire and tossed the hose on the grass.

"Oh, no. Did Timmy say something inappropriate again?" His mom glared at him, making him squirm.

"Oh, gosh no. He's been a little angel."

"Really?"

"Nic is having a hard day, so I wanted to see if I could take the kids down to the park and then get some ice cream."

"She's having a tough time still, huh?"

Claire nodded. Some days they just sailed through, others they walked on eggshells around Nic. Not because she unleashed her venom on them, but because she carried her pain alone and often secluded herself away in a separate bedroom. Once she'd been holed up for days. Claire had cracked the door just enough to check in on her and received only a firm, "I'm fine. I'll be out soon."

Two days later, Nic, worse for wear, finally came out and engaged with the world, but barely.

"I'm so sorry, Claire. Is there anything I can do?"

"I wish. It's the migraines. They come on without any warning and she struggles just to get to bed. The doctor said it would take time. The head trauma was extensive."

"I saw her the other day, outside with Grace, and I couldn't tell. Not like when she came home and had the stitches and everything." Jill moved her hand around her face and then grimaced. "Poor thing."

"Yeah, that's just it. Sometimes I forget 'cause she healed so quick and her scars are starting to fade." Claire smiled. "I'm sorry, I didn't mean to bore you with my stuff. I just wanted to come over and see if Timmy could come with us to the park and get ice cream later."

Jill looked at her watch. "You know what, dinner is almost ready, so why don't I take this little hellion off your hands and you and Grace can have some quiet time?"

Relieved, Claire conceded she could use a coffee and some quiet time with Grace. "Are you sure?"

"Ah, Mom. Ice cream." Timmy huffed.

"We have ice cream here."

"Not like the ice cream store."

She reached for his hand and walked him to the gate. "It's just like the ice cream store. I'll talk to you later, Claire. Tell Nic I'm sorry she's having a hard time."

"I will. Timmy, we'll go another time, promise."

Timmy just waved as his mom scooted him toward the house.

Claire knelt and looked at Grace. "Sorry Timmy couldn't go."

"It's okay." She moved closer to Claire's ear. "I was sorta sick of him. He's a ball hog."

"Oh, okay. Well, how about we go get you a hot chocolate and me a coffee, and we'll go to the beach and watch the ocean?"

"With whip cream?" Grace grabbed her mom's hand and skipped back to the house.

"Yep, with whipped cream."

"Sure. Besides, we can give Momma time to rest. She needs her beauty sleep. Lately she's been looking really tired."

Claire looked at her daughter in surprise. "Really?"

"Yeah," Grace said, climbing into the back seat and buckling in. "I heard her scream again last night."

"I'm sorry, honey. Did it scare you?"

Grace looked out the window and shook her head, wiping her nose on the back of her sleeve. "No, I'm used to it. Is she in pain, Mommy?"

"I don't think so. I think she's dreaming."

"You mean she's having a nightmare? 'Cause I scream when I have a nightmare, not a dream. What does Momma nightmare about?"

"You mean what causes her nightmares?"

Grace gave Claire that look that always cracked her up. It was such a grown-up look she couldn't handle it.

"I think she's having nightmares about her accident, honey."

"Maybe if I give her Matilda, she would stop nightmares about the accident."

Matilda was a soft cloth doll Nic had picked up at the airport in DC when she was finally allowed to leave the hospital. Nic had worried that Grace would be afraid of her with her stitches, bruises, and missing teeth, but it had gone better than either Claire or Nic had expected. Though she was wary of Nic and her bandages at first, once they established some sense of normalcy after a few days Grace had crawled up into Nic's lap and offered to kiss her boo-boos. Claire wished she'd had a camera to capture the special moment. Her daughter never ceased to surprise her with her loving, gentle nature.

"Could I have coffee, Mommy?"

That came out of left field. "Uh, no. You're too young for coffee, sweetie."

"Timmy's mom lets him have coffee. His dad says it will put hair on his chest."

"Do you want hair on your chest?" She looked at her daughter in the rearview mirror. Grace vehemently shook her head. "Okay, no hair on the chest then. Hot chocolate it is."

"With whip cream."

"With whipped cream. Deal."

Claire and Nic had discussed at length things like lattes, cell phones, and video games when it came to Grace. They'd agreed that she was too young, even if everyone else had them, and they were leery about the internet, too. So far, they had been able to distract her with outdoor activities, books, trips to the library, and chores. Limiting their own computer use made it easier to enforce the rules. Claire wasn't sure how much longer they would be able to keep the technology bug at bay, but they were willing to do it for as long as possible.

"Envision parking, sweetie," Claire said. It was a mantra she always invoked when she was praying to the parking gods. Monterey in general was notorious for the lack of parking, and downtown was worse. As "tourist season" had become a fiction in favor of a year-round reality, residents had to battle for parking on a daily basis with the ever-increasing swell of visitors.

"Okay." Grace scrunched her eyes closed and frowned.

"Is that your envisioning face?" Claire laughed.

Grace just nodded.

Claire circled the block twice before finally finding someone walking to his car. She rolled the window down.

"Are you leaving?"

The man gave her a thumbs-up before he got into his vehicles. She'd started doing that—alerting people that she was waiting—because lately it seemed so many drivers would get in, start their cars, and then sit checking their phones.

Frustrating.

Like clockwork, he started his car, put his blinker on, and the wait began.

Tick, tock. Tick, tock. Finally, he backed out and then gave her a wave.

"Asshole."

"Asshole," came from the backseat with the same inflection as Claire's invective.

"Grace…"

"What, Mommy?"

"You shouldn't talk like that."

"But you do."

"Hmm, Mommy's older and has earned the right to say a bad word sometimes, but I shouldn't."

"It's okay, Mommy. I think once in a while is okay."

Claire smiled. Her daughter was giving her permission to be bad. Life was funny at times.

"Thank you, honey." Claire lined herself up and tried to back into the parking space, then pulled forward and cursed. "Damn it. I fucking hate parallel parking." She turned and grabbed the passenger seat headrest to see behind her better, and noticed Grace had her fingers in her ears. She chuckled.

Finally jockeying the car into the slot, she grabbed the steering wheel and groaned in relief and frustration.

Let it go, she said over and over.

"It's okay, Mommy." Grace had unbuckled herself from her booster seat and was patting her mother on the shoulder. Then she planted a kiss on Claire's cheek and wrapped her arms around Claire's neck.

God, I love being a mom.

"Thank you, sweetie. Hot chocolate?"

"Okay," Grace yelled and pumped her fist.

Another gift from Timmy. It was so…Well, it didn't matter. If that was the worst thing she picked up from neighborhood kids, Claire and Nic would be lucky.

Morgan's Coffee Shop was always busy with locals

who had decided that supporting small businesses kept the big chain stores out of Monterey. The city council had recently caved and allowed two fast food chains to open on Alvarado, so it would eventually and inevitably let more chains in. Nearby Carmel's city council, on the other hand, never allowed chain stores and restaurants downtown, except for those with the cachet of Tiffany, Neiman Marcus, and a few other high-end stores. Claire guessed that image was everything to Carmelites. She preferred the lower-key vibe of Monterey.

"Mom, can I have a cookie?"

"Sure, honey. Which one?" Claire bent and looked inside the case filled with baked goodies.

"That one." She pointed to the biggest cookie covered in hard blue frosting.

"That's kinda big."

"I'm kinda big, Mommy. Besides, we could share it."

"Okay. That one, please." Claire pointed for the clerk.

Handing the cookie to Grace, she said, "There you go."

"Thank you."

Grabbing their drinks, Claire sat them outside. The sun would disappear around 3:00 p.m., so they needed to soak in as much Vitamin D as possible.

"I like this." Grace pointed to what was left of her cookie. The eaten part had left blue frosting all over her face.

"I can see that, sweetie." Claire wiped the crumbs from Grace's cheeks and chin, but it was going to take a good washcloth to get that color off.

"Mommy?"

"Hmm?"

"Is Momma going to be okay?"

Claire thought it a strange question to come from Grace. She should be worried about school, play, and eating her veggies. The idea that Nic was on her mind bothered Claire.

"Nic is going to be okay. You know how sometimes you get a headache when you eat ice cream too fast?"

Grace slid off her chair and stood at Claire's knee, then slapped her forehead with her palm. "Oh, man, that hurts."

"Well, that's what's happening to Nic right now. Her head hurts for a long time." She lifted Grace up on her lap and snuggled her.

"Oh, poor Momma. I'm gonna give her Matilda. When my tummy hurts, I put her on my tummy and she helps it stop hurting."

"That is so sweet of you, sweetie."

Grace was growing up to be so empathetic. Claire was proud of her daughter, especially considering the hardships she'd weathered so young in her life, like losing her father in the helicopter crash, moving and making new friends, and now school. Big steps in a little person's life.

"Should we go home and check on Nic?"

"Yes. She can have some of my cookie." Grace handed the cookie over to Claire, with only a few bites left. Claire had known the big treat would be too much for Grace.

"Okay, I'll just put it back in the bag and we'll take it home for Momma."

"Okay. Mommy, can we have a baby?"

"Ah, well…um…"

Isabella

Chapter One

Cece shoved a pile of jeans into the duffel and took a deep breath. She hated leaving Melita again. The only saving grace was that this was probably the last time she'd leave her behind.

"Mommy, I want to come with you." Melita's voice pierced Cece's heart. Peeking over the flap of the duffel, the girl shoved her favorite doll into the bag, trying to be subtle.

"Sweetie, you can't yet."

"Why?" The expression on her cherub face broke Cece.

"I have to find a place for us to live, and I don't have anyone to watch you yet."

Melita puffed up her chest, her hands on her hips. She bounced on the bed. "I'm big enough to watch myself."

Barely five, Melita looked old for her age and Cece had hardly recognized her little squirt when she'd come home from the police academy on the occasional leave days. Six months away had been hard, but the few weekends at home had made it almost tolerable.

Going back to her packing, Cece lamented how soon she had to leave. She wanted to make it to Monterey with enough time for a quick trip around the campus and to grab dinner. Grabbing a stack of T-shirts, she smiled at the open duffel. For every shirt and pants she put into the bag, she had to take out a stuffed animal or toy Melita had put in. She had to give it to her daughter—she was persistent.

"Someone has to take care of Nana until I come home to get you. Think you can do that for me?"

"Moooom." Melita dragged out the "O" for a good three seconds.

"Honey, Mommy is in a hotel until housing is ready for us," she said, stuffing more clothes into the duffel. Thank god her new uniform and utility belt were already hanging in the truck waiting for the last of her few meager possessions. Living in the military and constantly moving had taught her that things were replaceable. Her most prized possession would be safely nestled in the arms of her mother until Cece could retrieve Melita and bring her to Monterey.

"Mommy?"

"Yes."

"Could you stop for a minute? I want to talk to you."

"Sweetie, I have to get up to Monterey before it gets dark."

"Please?"

Cece stopped and sat on the bed, pulling her daughter onto her lap. "Okay. What did you want to talk about?"

Melita put her hands on each side of Cece's face and squished her cheeks into their signature fish-lips face. Cece was having a tough time leaving Melita home this time. Just turning five, she was getting ready to start kindergarten and South-Central LA was nowhere to raise a child. She should know; this was where she'd grown up and it wasn't where she wanted to raise her daughter. The neighborhood hadn't just changed, it was decidedly more violent. Girls were joining gangs, and drugs and guns were everywhere. Hell, when she first arrived home from the academy, she'd had to pass through a makeshift gauntlet of men sitting in lawn chairs blocking her street. Luckily one of those men had been her little brother, Santino. He was anything but a saint.

"Cece? What the fuck? What are you doing here? I didn't know you were coming home."

Cece regarded the three other men. One sported a baseball bat, one a pipe, and she was sure they were all packing. Looking up at Santino, she couldn't miss how skinny he was. His clean, pristinely white T-shirt draped off on him like it was on a hanger. It hid the two bullet holes that had almost taken his life. It was a miracle he'd survived, earning him the nickname Angelito—Guardian Angel. He'd taken the bullets meant for another gang member, so now he was not only a martyr, he was angelic. A few new tattoos littered his arms, and a cigarette hung from his lips.

"What's going on, Santino? I want to go home, but your guys are blocking the street."

He nodded his head back at the crew sitting in the lawn chairs and suddenly the street was cleared for her to go through.

"We're just protecting what's ours, sis."

"For fuck's sake, Santino." She didn't wait for a reply as she cranked on the wheel and turned to go down her street. "This is some bullshit right here," she said, looking at one of the stocky men waving her through. "Just my luck I'll get shot and killed here and not in a fucking hot zone like Afghanistan." She watched Santino jog back to his chair and take up his position sitting between the other men.

She hated LA. The traffic was awful, there were

too many people, and the gangs had chewed up the neighborhood and spit out garbage. If the older residents didn't die, they moved away to bedroom communities to be with children who themselves had left for safer pastures, only to be replaced with those looking for cheap houses or rent, mistaking the neighborhood for something they were used to back home. Little did they know they were only providing the next generation of gang members as the kids desperate to fit in—or be protected—joined the gangs.

It was a vicious cycle that had claimed her best friend, Melita. They were walking home after a high school dance with a group of kids when a car sped around a corner. Two guys hung out the window and shot at the group. Melita had been standing in front of Cece when it all happened. It sounded like firecrackers exploding, so no one had really been spooked. Then the kids started to drop and Melita had fallen against Cece, clutching her stomach.

Blood was everywhere.

Kids were screaming and running, leaving Cece sitting on the sidewalk holding Melita. The last thing she remembered was Melita's brown eyes staring at her, mouthing, "Help me."

Now her brother Santino sat in a lawn chair acting like some kind of overlord, watching over *his* street.

"Mija, are you okay?" Her mother's sweet, gentle voice pulled her from the wretched memory.

"I'm good, Mom. Just thinking about the move."

Sitting next to her, her mother took her hand. "It's going to be okay."

She leaned her head on her mother's shoulder. "I know. I just can't wait until we're all out of this neighborhood."

Her mother stroked her hair and kissed the top of her head. "At least you're home safe now."

"Mommy, I want to go with you. Tell her, Nana, I'm big enough to take care of myself." Melita wedged between the two women and hugged them both.

"Don't be in such a hurry to grow up, Lita," her grandmother said. "You're just like your mommy. She wanted to be all grown up, too."

"But I—"

"Why don't you go and get a soda, Lita?"

Melita looked at her mother with a questioning glance.

"Yes, you can have half a soda. I don't want you wetting the bed tonight."

"Mommy, I don't wet the bed anymore."

"Okay, then I don't want you awake at all hours of the night and keeping your grandmother up."

Walking away, Melita said, "I won't. Geez."

"What's really bothering you, Cece?"

"I'm tired of leaving you both behind." She took advantage of the time Lita was gone and stuffed her duffel with the last few items and then snapped it closed. "I want you to move up to Monterey, Mom."

"Honey—"

"I'm not taking no for an answer. I don't want you here by yourself anymore. Besides, you'll be with us and I could really use your help with Melita. You don't want a stranger raising your granddaughter, do you?" She knew that would get a reaction, even if it was just the silent treatment.

"What about Santino? He needs me."

"Mom, he doesn't need you except to raid the fridge or for some quick cash. If you haven't noticed, he's a grown man and should be taking care of himself. Besides, you deserve to take care of yourself, be safe, and not have to worry about the next drive-by shooting. He doesn't stay here, does he?"

"Oh, only once in a while."

Tossing her leather jacket on, she shouldered her duffel. She knew he only stayed with their mother when he was running from something, or someone.

"Mom, I'm a cop now and I can't have you or Melita in danger. He doesn't give a shit about your safety."

"Cece, you know that's not true."

"No? Then why would he stay with you, knowing that he could be a target for some little punk trying to make a name for himself?"

"Honey, aren't you exaggerating just a little?"

"No, Mom, I'm not. Haven't you seen him and his goons sitting at the end of the block keeping people from coming down the street? It's ridiculous. Nobody lives like that outside of South Central. It's a fucking war zone here. I felt safer in Afghanistan than I do here."

Her mother shot her the "bullshit" look she was famous for when Cece was growing up. Cece was on the receiving end of that look every time she told a half truth.

"It's true, Mom."

"Have you forgotten that you were wounded your last deployment?"

"I haven't forgotten, Mom. But I walked out of that hospital with my life. Here, there are no guarantees." Cece stuffed her wallet, pocketknife, and money in her backpack. "I want you to at least consider it. Dad is gone, there isn't any family here except me, Melita, and Santino. Once Melita and I move to Monterey, you'll be here all by yourself and I won't be able to come down for a while." Cece got on her knees in front of her mother, then took her hands and squeezed them.

"Please promise me that you will come. Melita needs you, but more importantly, I need you. We've been apart for too long, and now that I'm home, I want us to be together." She brought her mother's hands to her lips and kissed them. They were soft but had been strong enough to discipline two wild kids and make a living when her dad got sick, and now, she placed her daughter's life in them.

"Please."

"Tell you what. I'll come up and get Melita ready for school and help out for a little while, and then we can see how it goes. It's been a long time since we two strong women lived under one roof. I remember when your father's mother came to live with us." She wrinkled her nose. "That woman was a bear to live with."

"I remember," Cece said, standing and pulling her mother up with her. Wrapping her in a hug, she squeezed her tight. "I better go. I've got a long drive and I want to try and beat the traffic out of town."

"Mommy, want a drink?" Melita walked in and shoved the soda at her mom.

"Sure, pumpkin."

"I didn't spit in it."

Cece looked at her mom and grimaced. "Good to know." Taking a small drink, she handed it back to Melita, shouldered her backpack, scooped up her duffel with one hand, and reached out to Melita with the other. "Walk me out to my truck?"

Silently, the trio navigated the small two-bedroom house and out to her truck. This was the hardest part of any visit. At least she knew this would be the last time she'd have to do it for a while.

She tossed her stuff on the passenger seat and peeked back into the crew cab, making sure her uniform was still there. Grabbing it off the seat, she hung it up on the hook. Now that she was leaving, she didn't have to worry about someone seeing it and taking a potshot at it during the night. It was like a neon sign telling the local bangers that a cop lived there. Her mom didn't need that kind of hassle. She didn't care if Santino got hassled over it—he could handle it.

"Okay, give me a kiss, kiddo." Cece reached down and hoisted Melita up for a hug.

"Here, give me that, Lita, so you can give your mommy a proper hug."

"Kay." She handed over the can and wrapped her arms around Cece's neck and squeezed.

Cece's heart sank. It was never easy saying good-bye to her daughter. When she was younger, Melita would give a quick peck on the cheek and run off to play with her friends. That hurt more than this did, but this time it was different. Melita had begged to come, and she'd had to tell her daughter no.

"Lita, can you play?" A little girl riding her bike pulled into the driveway.

"Nana?"

"Go, sweetie. Stay out of the street," Cece answered instead, putting her down and swatting her butt.

"I love you, Mommy." She grabbed the can of soda from her grandmother, then turned to her mother. "Can I have a phone, Mommy?"

"What? No." Cece laughed at the sudden change

in direction.

"Laura has one. Why can't I have one?"

"We'll talk about it later, and don't go begging your grandmother for one, okay?"

"Okay," Melita said, dejected. She recovered quickly as she raced over to her pink bike, putting her soda in the drink holder that was attached to the handlebars.

"Who put that on there?"

"Santino. He said she needs to have her hands free when she rode. So, he put it on."

"Hmmm. He doesn't hang around her, does he?"

"Cece. He is her tío."

"Yeah, yeah. I don't want her going anywhere with him. Okay?"

"Go. You've got a long drive and the traffic is only going to get worse the later it gets."

"It's nine in the morning, Mom. The traffic should be clearing up." She kissed her mom on the cheek and slid into the driver's seat. "I love you, Mom."

Her mom rubbed her arm and smiled down at her. "I love you too, honey. Call us when you get to Monterey."

"I will. Bye, Lita," she yelled to her daughter, trying to catch her attention.

Melita stopped in the middle of the sidewalk and blew her mom a kiss. Cece made a grabbing motion and gobbled the kiss.

"Watch out for her, Mom. She sure seems fearless lately."

Her mother looked over at Melita. "She is your daughter."

"Yep." Slapping the side of her truck, she said, "I gotta go. I'll call. Love you."

Pulling out of the driveway, she watched her mom and Melita disappear in her rearview mirror. Her heart ached at another leaving. It never got easier for her, but she knew this would be the last time if the trip to Monterey turned out to be everything she hoped.

⁂

Interstate 5 puked out commuters down the hill on the north side of the Tejon Pass, known to locals as the Grapevine. Wide-open spaces replaced cities crammed to the gills with stuff. People stuff—cars, clothes, restaurants that served fusion this or that, coffee shops on every corner, and more cars. While the traffic could be a bitch to get through, even with all three and sometimes four lanes cruising at above highway speed, it was a different world on the other side of the Grapevine.

It seemed everyone was either in a hurry to get out of LA or speeding to get to it, with its seductive siren song to wannabe starlets, models, and those just looking to hang with the rich and famous. Maybe Cece was a tad cynical. She'd met a few wannabes and just didn't see the allure of fame and fortune. Give her enough money to pay her bills, raise her daughter, and put gas in her tank, and she was good to go. Relentless, pounding, stinging sand blowing in her face had straightened her priorities. She'd seen how others lived in what amounted to mud huts with dirt floors. Those people, who found it impossible to understand American values and wanted her dead, lived a simple existence. Joy wasn't an emotion she saw a lot of on their faces. Survival—now that she recognized in them. That was universal. Not the glitz and glamor of

Hollywood.

The clear blue sky, the agricultural fields as far as the eye could see, no people in sight…Maybe it was the allure of a world with fewer people that Cece craved for herself and Melita. A calm feeling came over her as she looked for the transition to stay on I-5.

Cece glanced around the car for the care package her mother always snuck into the truck's cab when she left. A brown paper bag sat between the duffel and her console, next to it a small doll. She instantly recognized it as one Melita had tried to tuck away in her bag earlier. Picking it up she folded the doll's legs and placed her on the dash of her pickup. That way she would think of Lita every time she saw it.

Reaching in the bag, she pulled out a sandwich with a note taped to the wrapper.

Sweetheart,

I'm so proud of you. Be safe and call when you get to Monterey.

Love,
Mom

Her mom took an old-school approach to communication. While Cece appreciated that her mom did her best to text and send an occasional email, it was the handwritten letters she received when deployed that had really brightened her day. They held a special place in her heart and were neatly gathered in a box that she'd already packed to take to Monterey. While most of the guys fought for face time with their wives and kids, she was content to read her letters and look at all her pictures when seeking a taste of home and the comfort that brought. Her mother always included positive little sayings and inspirations in her letters along with something homemade.

She hoped she could carry on the same motherly traditions like notes in Melita's lunches, stories at night, and cuddles on the weekends. All the little things that made a mother, a mom.

The phone rang through her stereo and the name made her smile. She wondered if her mother's ears were burning or if they just had that psychic connection.

"Hi, Mom."

"Hi, Mommy."

"Hi, sweetheart. Everything okay?"

"Yeah…" Her daughter's voice didn't sound like everything was okay.

"What's wrong?"

"Margaret says I don't have a real mommy," Lita said through sobs.

"What? Of course, you have a real mommy. I'm your mommy."

Cece hated kids sometimes. She could easily be a tractor parent, but she wasn't home to bulldoze over those little shits. It would be different when she moved Melita up north, she kept reminding herself.

"I know."

The gentle sobs broke Cece's heart. "Honey, let me talk to Nana."

"Kay. Here, Nana. Mommy wants to talk to you."

"Hi, sweetheart."

"What happened, Mom?"

"You know how kids can be, Cece."

"Don't let her play with Margaret, Mom."

"Honey—"

"Mom, I'm serious. She doesn't need this shit. Not right now."

"Lita will be okay. Besides, I told her I would take her out for ice cream after dinner. I've got her favorite movie in right now, and I'll bet she'll have forgotten all about it in a few minutes."

"God, this sucks." Cece was tempted to turn around and pick up Lita and bring her with her to Monterey. Screw the lack of daycare. She could almost bet Claire could help her find someone to help with Lita's care until they got settled.

"Don't you dare come back here." Her mom was beyond a mind reader; she knew exactly what Cece was thinking most of the time. Mom ESP, she called it. Another trait Cece could only hope would be hereditary.

"You know me too well, Mom."

"No, I just know what I would want to do if someone was messing with my daughter. You have to let her fight her own battles sometimes, honey. She has to learn to stand up for herself. I had to learn to let you do the same, and my mom gave me the exact same advice, too."

"Hmm."

"She'll be okay. As long as she knows she can call you, it will help. Trust me."

"Okay. Not too much ice cream, though."

"Honey, one of the perks of being a grandmother is the ability to spoil my only grandchild with hugs and ice cream when the moment calls for them."

"I know, Mom. I know. Okay."

Her GPS broke through their conversation. "Take the right two lanes for I-5."

"That's my turn, Mom. I'll call you when I stop

in Lost Hills for gas."

"Try not to worry, honey. She's already lost in the movie."

"Okay, okay. Give her a hug for me and tell her I'll call when I get to Monterey."

"Drive carefully, and we'll talk later."

"Thanks, Mom."

"Of course, sweetheart."

"Later."

"Bye."

The line went dead. Cece gritted her teeth. Looking at the GPS, she was three and a half hours from her destination but a lifetime from where she really wanted and needed to be. Her return trip to bring her daughter home wouldn't be soon enough, but she was building a new life and it wasn't something she would compromise on. It was too important for Melita.

She pulled the sandwich out of its wrapper. Turkey with Swiss on plain white bread. Her mom knew her too well.

Chapter Two

$\mathcal{C}$laire's finger traced out an invisible trail between Nic's breasts, then around a nipple, and finally up her neck, stopping on Nic's lips. Nic kissed the tip and then bit the end, holding it between her teeth.

"Careful there, tiger…" Claire said as Nic's hips jerked suggestively against hers. She planted another kiss on the swollen lips and slowly let her hand travel down the curve of her hip, detouring around and between Nic's legs. "You might start something you can't finish."

There, she'd thrown down the challenge. It had taken everything she had to get Nic into their bed. Claire was growing weary of the separate bedrooms, but she understood her wife's reasons. The first few weeks Nic had been home and sleeping in their bed she had thrashed around so violently that Claire ended up with a black eye and a split lip. Luckily, she'd just taken a sleeping Grace to her own room and had avoided their daughter being caught in Nic's unintentional nocturnal melee.

Nic cocked a grin and threaded her fingers in Claire's hair, pulling her closer and crushing Claire's lips against her own. Rolling Claire onto her back, she dove in and ran her tongue along the pulse that was racing in her neck before settling down to gently nibble.

Claire's body bucked under Nic's. This time Claire put her hands over her head and grabbed the headboard of the bed as her hips rolled under Nic. She was giving total control to Nic, and she hoped Nic wouldn't waste it. It was her way of surrendering to her lover without blatantly telling her.

She'd noticed recently that Nic had a harder time processing subtle little hints she left like breadcrumbs for her to follow. Getting intimate now with Nic involved a whole lot of planning and praying that she'd pick up those hints. Sometimes she saw the lightbulb flicker in Nic's eyes, but more often than not it took a ball-peen hammer to the temples to bring Nic around. Lately, she'd resolved to just come right out and say she needed to reconnect with her wife and wanted sex. Subtlety be damned.

She wouldn't waste this moment; they were fewer and even farther between than two women on their periods marking Xs on the calendar to line up their "monthlies."

Her clit tingled as her mind went back to where her body had been for the last few minutes. God, she couldn't get enough of her lover, and once Nic was on board for the physical intimacy, there was no quenching her thirst. Hands had moved in unison as they touched each other and removed the rest of their clothing at a fever pitch. Every time they were alone like this it was like the house was on fire and they only had a few minutes to squeeze in a quickie. Nic had been like someone whose death sentence was inevitable. Claire had tried to slow her down, but the look in Nic's eyes told her the need to connect was greater than her need to breathe, to be joined together in an abyss that lacked words and seeing. Like two blind women, they reached for parts that were memorized from years of lovemaking sessions. Urgency always seemed to be the word of the moment.

⚜⚜⚜⚜

Nic lay spent, cradling Claire.

"Let's get married before you go back to work," Claire said.

"Huh? We are married. Remember?" Nic lifted her left hand and wiggled her fingers. The basic band with small diamonds circling it caught what little light there was in the room and sparkled.

Claire snuggled closer and rested her leg across Nic's hips. "A wedding. You promised we'd have a wedding when you got back from Afghanistan."

"A wedding?"

"Are you dodging the idea, Nicole?"

Claire was bringing out the big guns, using her full name. Now, she meant business, and Nic wouldn't be able to get out of the discussion.

"Your scars are healed, your dental work is almost done, and the semester will eventually end. I can't think of anything I'd rather do than spend the next few months planning a wedding."

"Really? You want to plan a wedding with your current class load?"

"The semester is ending, silly. I have the summer to plan. Think of it: Grace, Jordan, and I can put on the wedding of the century."

"The century?" Nic laughed.

"Okay, how about a kick-ass party where you and I can exchange our vows with twenty of our closest friends?"

"If that will make you happy, it makes me happy."

Nic turned toward Claire and ran her finger along her cheek, pushing a few strands of hair back. She felt her lover smiling in the dark just before Claire playfully grabbed Nic's hand and kissed her palm.

She struggled to come to terms with how close she'd come to losing all of this several months back. While her physical scars were healing, her heart and soul were taking longer to adjust to a new reality, one where she was on constant alert, where venturing outside to the doctor, the dentist, and to group therapy became an exercise in diligence. Something as simple as a car backfiring practically put her in the fetal position, but she'd be damned if she'd show it. This wasn't who she sought to be, and it certainly wasn't the person Claire wanted as her partner and the parent Grace deserved. Maybe a wedding was the gradual ramp back into social activity she needed.

"It'll be fun. Besides, Jordan can help. You know how she has a flair for fashion and design." Claire gently pulled Nic's chin toward her. "She'll take the place of the bride's mother and be in the middle of everything. You won't have to lift a finger."

"That sounds great, sweetheart." Nic hoped she sounded more encouraging that she felt.

She had time to help before going back to the mundane world of work. Who knew work would sound so wonderful? She was ready to get back into the flow of a nine-to-five life. She had an appointment to speak to the commandant of Naval Postgraduate, and with any luck she'd be teaching by fall. Her dream job was at her fingertips. All she needed to do was tap it and take it.

She hoped.

"I'm hungry. How about you?" Claire stood and wrapped the sheet around her body, covering the best parts as far as Nic was concerned. At least her desire for Claire hadn't waned. It had stumbled a few times when she got home, but a broken jaw and facial scars didn't exactly make her feel attractive enough to think about sex. Regardless of how many times Claire said differently, it just didn't compute for Nic.

"What did you have in mind?" Nic tugged at the sheet, pulling Claire back on top of her. "I could eat again, but I'm not sure food is on the menu." She offered Claire the most lecherous smile she could muster with her new lopsided grin.

Peeling the rest of the sheet off, Claire rhythmically rolled her hips on her lover's body.

Nic had fantasized about moments like this while overseas, but those never compared to having the real thing in her hands, no matter how kinky her dreams were. Her palms glided over nipples that hardened at the contact. She closed her eyes, letting her touch create the memory of now, for later. Lips topped hers, caressing and then darting between, begging to be let in. She threaded her fingers through Claire's hair and held her close, her mouth dominating and controlling. She stilled Claire's hips and held them again her as her body started to seize at the start of an orgasm. Rolling Claire over, she bucked her hips against Claire's and pressed herself again between her open legs. Rubbing against the wetness, Claire gasped in her ear as she started to vibrate through her own orgasm against Nic.

Nic woke with a start. For a moment she didn't recognize the room. Claire's room, not their room. She was trapped by the weight of Claire's body. The way it held her down made her mind race and she started to panic. It took all she had not to toss Claire off her and run. Her body felt like it was on fire, bombs going off around her, sand in her mouth, spitting teeth, smoke burning her nostrils as she pulled air in. She had to stop, now, before she was in a full-blown panic attack.

She remembered the therapist's words: "Focus on your breathing, Nic."

She closed her eyes and took a deep breath.

Exhaled.

Took another deep breath.

Exhaled.

She thought of the beach. The crashing waves. Anything but that day in Afghanistan.

Slipping out from under Claire, she pulled her sweats on, shoved her feet into her slippers, and plodded back to her room. Her room, not their room.

The blackness was a shroud that protected Nic. Like her uniform, it allowed Nic to compartmentalize the pain. She shoved all of it in a box to be dissected later when she sat in the therapist's office where she struggled to pull everything out. It was there, she just didn't know how to give it voice, to be vulnerable and weak. The prodding, the bargaining, and the silent approach didn't work. Oftentimes she'd sat in the office memorizing the books on the shelf or counting the homey knickknacks that lined the desk. All designed to put a client at ease, she was sure. Funny how an hour seemed to drag when two people just sat and waited for the other person to talk. She'd had more fun having a root canal than having her head shrunk. Maybe she still wasn't ready to purge the dreadful memories. They, too, had become something she hid behind in a strange, grotesque sort of way. A nightmare that was trotted out when it felt like running free, not when she wanted to exorcise it. The damn demon sat on her shoulder and laughed at her, shoving its pitchfork in her ear from time to time to remind her it was still around at the most inopportune times, like now.

She stood at the window fingering the heavy curtains that protected her from the outside. If she were playing shrink, she'd imagine that they symbolized a barrier between her and the real world, something that could hide her scars from prying eyes. All she wanted to do was throw them wide open and let the light shine on the real Nic. But she couldn't.

She threw herself into the overstuffed wingback chair and buried her face in her hands. The walls were closing in on her. Claustrophobia was setting in. Her chest tightened within the constraints as she felt the room easing downward.

Breathe.

She rocked herself back and forth.

Breathe.

Things were great when she'd first returned home. Familiar surroundings, their daughter Grace, and dealing with rehab had consumed her life in the beginning. Reintegration seemed to be seamless at first. Lately, though, as hard as she tried, the bombing had seeped into her life. At first it was an occasional nightmare here and there. Then there was what should have been a simple outing with Claire. A car backfiring had her jumping out of her skin, but she switched into sheepdog mode, gathering her family together and looking around for a quick exit to keep them safe. Her mind raced, adrenaline pumped through her body, and she couldn't seem to process rationally even though she knew she was Stateside and not in the sand dunes of Afghanistan. Her priority was to protect her family at all costs. They had replaced her squad and her concerns now that she was home.

Claire had picked up on it immediately and pulled the car off the road to the side, put it in Park, and held Nic until she could calm down. She wanted to curl up in the fetal position until it all went away, but her logical side told her that she was the protector. But her insides were churning, ready to heave her meager breakfast. Sweat beaded up all over her body and her head swam, a precursor to blacking out. She pushed away from Claire and straightened up.

"I'm okay. It's just a reflex reaction," Nic explained.

"It's okay, sweetheart. You don't have to be brave for me. I know what happened over there. You're safe." Claire slid closer to Nic and tried to comfort her.

Nic flinched at the contact. "I'm okay, honey. Really. Can we go? I have a ton of stuff to get done and it was just a reaction to the sound. I'm fine." She grabbed for Claire's hand as Claire withdrew. Bringing it to her lips, she kissed the knuckles. "Seriously, I'm okay."

Then the nightmares returned every night. After one exceptionally bad night when she unknowingly hit Claire in the face, Nic started sleeping in the spare bedroom. She couldn't risk hitting her wife again. It had crushed her when it happened.

"Jesus, Claire, are you all right?" Nic had cupped Claire's face in the darkness. She could feel tears streaming down her wife's cheeks. "I'm so sorry. I can't believe this is happening."

"What's going on, honey? Things seem to be going along just fine and suddenly it's like…I know, I'm not an expert, but something's happened."

Nic held Claire close. Afraid to let her go, all she could do was offer a paltry apology. "I don't know, it seems like things are just…" The truth was, she didn't know what was going on with her anymore.

"Things are what?" Claire twisted out of her arms and straddled Nic's hips. Claire had clutched Nic to her breast and rocked her like a child. In an odd sort of way, it was comforting. Their roles had been flipped ever since Germany. Claire had swooped in and taken control of her care and the travel arrangements back to the States, all while still taking care of Grace and buying a house. Nic was constantly amazed by Claire's ability to find a silver lining in even the darkest cloud.

"It's going to be okay," Claire had whispered in Nic's ear. She gently ran her fingers through Nic's hair and kissed the top of her head. "It's time for a haircut, sweetheart."

Nic had leaned back and looked up in her lover's eyes. "What would I do without you?"

"I'm not going to let you find out." Claire had said, smiling.

Breathe, Nic told herself. *Just breathe.* Nic leaned back against the chair, gripping its arms, her fingers practically digging through the upholstery.

Transitioning to the real world was taking more time than she expected, but more importantly transitioning back to a wife was harder. After Nic's injury the last time she was in Iraq, she'd learned to deal with the pain on her own. A little counseling and lots of medical care moved her forward in her recovery, but she didn't have someone at home waiting for her then like she did now. It had been a big adjustment for Nic when Claire had come to the hospital in DC unexpectedly. Unlike her first recovery when Nic had no one to talk to about what had happened, this time Claire was there, waiting patiently to hear about every detail. A wired jaw, a busted orbital socket, not enough functioning brain cells, and a doctor who had insisted that Claire be prepared for slower responses had kept Claire by her side but also at bay, at least for a while.

Once Nic had come home, Claire had picked up the slack when Nic's PTSD kicked in and left her almost comatose. The dark abyss Nic found herself in at those times wasn't something Nic wanted to share with Claire; her wife had enough to deal with when Nic sequestered herself behind the dark façade she rarely had control over. So, like tonight, she relegated herself to the cool comfort the guest room—*her* room—offered her. Behind its strong door and heavy curtains, she could lose herself and give in to the darkness that engulfed her, if only for a moment.

A moment that was at the same time both too long and painfully too brief.

Chapter Three

Cece pulled into the motel she'd be living in for the next month, at least. The Travelers was more of a long-term stay than a motel. A few construction trucks littered the parking lot, a sight the manager told her was one she should get used to seeing as the workers' jobsite was only a few blocks away and not due to complete for another several weeks. All she cared about was a quiet place to sleep with little intrusion.

Keys in hand, she offloaded her bags and decided to give Nic a quick call, as promised.

"Hey, Nic. It's Cece."

"Hey, about time. Are you here?"

"Yep, just got here and am calling as promised."

"Great, come on over. You got here just in time. We're having a barbeque tonight and I want you to join us."

"Now?"

"Well, do you need a nap?"

Cece thought about it. She could definitely use a shower and some shut-eye.

"Well…I don't want to impose. I'm sure Claire—"

"Hey, Claire, Cece's here."

"Great, tell her to come over. Did she bring Melita with her?" Claire said in the background.

"Did you bring the little rugrat with you?"

"Not this trip."

"No, rug rat," she heard Nic yell to Claire. "No matter, just get your butt over here and let's eat."

"Are you sure?'

"Of course I'm sure."

Nic had become a close friend after the accident. She was part of the reason Cece had taken the job at Cal State Monterey Bay. Nic had encouraged Cece to consider retirement from the military but hadn't taken her own advice. Last they'd talked she'd told Cece the teaching spot she'd wanted before being shipped to Afghanistan had finally opened up, thanks to the retirement of the commandant who had made her life miserable before her deployment. It hadn't taken much to push Cece toward retirement, and her visit to the coast had sealed the deal.

"All right let me grab a quick shower and I'll be over. What can I bring?"

"Nothing, just get your butt over here. It will be great to see you again."

"Give me a half an hour."

❧❧❧❧

Cece tried to remember how to get to Nic's house. She'd been there once before when she visited CSUMB for her job interview, but she needed to learn the streets, especially since this was going to be her new home base. What stuck her most about this part of California were the open spaces. Traffic was light, the houses were spread apart, and the climate was much cooler than LA and definitely not as hot as when she was pounding sand overseas. This time, if she wanted sand it included a bathing suit, a towel, and a ten-minute drive where she could dig her toes into the wet sand and the brisk waters of the Pacific Ocean.

Pulling onto Nic's street, the first thing she noticed was the yellow sign on the side of the road that alerted people to children playing. Yep, she wasn't in LA anymore. She smiled as she recognized Nic's SUV halfway down the street. She had to pat herself on the back for remembering the way.

Parking in front of the house, she gave herself a minute to center herself. The last time she'd seen her friend, Nic hadn't been in the best of shape. A walker sat in the corner of the house, but Nic had refused to use it, opting for a cane instead. She had to give it to Nic, she was a determined woman. That's probably why they had hit if off in Afghanistan. That, and the fact that Nic had saved her life after the explosion. Cece had a broken collar bone and a few other injuries, but nothing compared to what Nic had endured.

Grabbing the bottle of wine and the six-pack of beer, she got out of the car. Reaching into the back seat, she picked up the stuffed bear she'd bought for Grace. She couldn't forget the little munchkin who'd wrapped herself around Cece when she found out Cece had a daughter, too. She was glad Nic had someone to come home to. It definitely made going home easier. At least it did for her.

Before she could even hit the doorbell, the door swung wide open.

"Hey, it's about time you got here."

Cece held up the gifts. "I couldn't come empty-handed," she said, handing Nic the wine and beer.

"You didn't have to bring anything. Hell, I'm just glad to see ya. Claire, Cece's here."

"Cece, did you have any problems finding the place?"

"Naw, easy peasy. Thanks for the invite, Claire." Cece kissed Claire on the cheek and smiled. "I brought a little something for Grace. I hope you don't mind."

Claire looked at the bear. "She's going to love it." Looking past Cece, she frowned. "Remind me, where is Melita?"

"Oh, I'm staying in a hotel. My mom's got her until I find a suitable place to live. Besides, I start work tomorrow and I don't have anything set up for her yet."

"Oh right, well we could've taken care of her."

"I appreciate that, Claire, but I wouldn't think of imposing."

"Oh, gosh, Cece, it wouldn't be an imposition."

Cece shrugged. "Thanks."

"Come on in. I was just starting the grill. I hope you're hungry, 'cause I'm starving." Nic led Cece through the kitchen toward the backyard.

"I'll bring out a couple of beers and nibbles." Claire wiped her hands on her apron and took the wine and beer from Nic.

"Nibbles, huh?" Cece smiled at Nic.

"She doesn't get a chance to entertain, so just humor her."

"It's sweet."

Nic winked at Cece and smiled. "I am a lucky gal, buddy." She slapped Cece on the back and opened the slider to the backyard.

"Nice," Cece said, taking in the backyard. "You scored, man."

"You like it? We've still got a little more work to get it where I want it, but it's coming along, slowly."

Nic offered Cece a seat on the deck and opened the grill. "Steak okay?"

"Seriously, I was gonna stop by a sub shop and

have a sandwich for dinner, so anything homemade is great."

Cece plopped down in the lawn chair and sighed. "How was the drive?"

"Oh, fine. Getting out of LA is always an adventure, but once I got past the Grapevine it was easy sailing." Her hand glided down for effect. "I realized how much I hate that city. Too many people, too many cars, and too many idiots stuck on stupid."

"Gotcha." Nic sat in the chair next to her. "Yeah, Monterey is nothing like the big city. Is it gonna be enough for ya?"

"Are you kidding me? I love it already."

Claire stepped through the door with two beers and a plate of food, napkins, and small plates.

Cece jumped up. "Here, let me help you with that." Cece grabbed the food and plates.

"Thanks." Claire shot Nic a look. "At least someone has some manners."

"What? I'm barbecuing." Nic laughed.

"Uh-huh." Claire playfully slapped at Nic. "You get to help with cleanup," she said, passing the beers to Nic.

"Okay, okay." Nic held up her hands in defeat.

"You can just put those on that table between you gals. I'm sure you're probably starving. Word of warning, don't let Nic hog all the food. She's got quite the appetite lately." Bending over Nic, she kissed her. "Right, honey?"

"Uh-huh," Nic said between kisses before Claire left.

"Where's Grace?"

"Taking a nap."

"Ah. I love nap time."

Nic handed a beer to Cece and they knocked bottles. "Cheers."

"Salud. So, how's life treating you? You look good." Cece sat and took a long sip of her beer.

"Yeah. I…feel good."

They sat in silence, looking over the backyard. She still thought of Nic as Colonel, so she didn't want to overstep.

"Are you back to work?"

"Not yet. I start back for the fall semester."

"That's great." She knew Nic wanted to teach, so obviously she was heading in the right direction with her rehab. "You ready?"

⚜⚜⚜⚜

"As ready as I'm going to be."

Nic wanted to be candid with Cece about how she was dealing with her PTSD. In fact, she wanted to ask how Cece was handling it, considering Cece's multiple tours overseas. Opening up wasn't her strongest suit, and Claire could attest to it. Her shrink had also told her that while their working together would help Nic, there was going to be a time when she needed to be around others who'd had similar experiences as Nic. Through those shared experiences she would see that she wasn't alone in the way she was dealing with things or the way she was feeling.

"Can I ask you a question?" Nic looked over at Cece.

"Sure, shoot." Cece flinched. "Sorry, bad metaphor. You can ask me anything, Colonel."

Nic smiled at the slip and Cece shrugged. "Sorry, old habits take time to die a good death."

"Don't worry. Besides, I don't think I have anything to fear from you, do I?" Nic winked at Cece, took a deep breath, and decided to venture out onto the ledge. "How's your PTSD?"

Cece coughed and took another sip of her beer. Clearing her throat, she said. "Are you struggling, Nic?"

Nic searched Cece's face expecting some sort of judgment, but all she saw was concern. "I have my moments. You don't struggle with it at all?"

"I didn't say that. I did, at first, but I've been there so many times that you sort of get used to living on alert. I've seen guys get their faces blown off, I've carried off my guys in a litter thinking they were going to live and then see them die before we could get back to the evac site." Cece sipped her beer and continued. "Everything seemed like a bad dream. First Iraq, then Afghanistan. At some point you close yourself off from those feelings. At least I did. It was the only way I thought I could survive the multiple deployments."

"So, why did you go back? I mean you've been injured before, so why put your life at risk again?"

"You need to ask Uncle Sam that question."

"Yeah, but you could have rejected re-enlisting again. I mean, that was your choice, right?" Nic put her hand up. "Sorry if I'm getting too personal. I mean we all make choices that—"

"We have to live with? Sure. I had a kid and I needed to be able to take care of my family. I had to help my mom out since my brother isn't very dependable, and Melita was young enough I thought the timing was better than when she'd be a teenager. I didn't have a lot of options, and I already had the skills and experience they were looking for from my first tour."

Nic looked out at the backyard and suddenly wished she'd kept her mouth shut. Cece wasn't just a stand-up gal, she was responsible and deserved respect for the decisions she made, just like every other servicemember out there who saw enlisting as a way up and out of their communities.

"Did you get counseling?"

"Well, I saw a priest on base for a while. You know, that whole life-and-death thing. I struggled at first with killing another human being."

Nic suddenly realized that Cece's experiences were immensely different than hers. Cece had to hump an M4 and protect her squad. All Nic had to do in her service to her country was fly a chopper or, on her last tour, interview tribal elders. Their final experience was a shared one, but Cece had more street cred with her multiple tours.

Cece put her hand on Nic's arm. "You okay, buddy?"

"Yeah. I just realized that your experiences are much vaster than mine."

"Vaster maybe, but not less than. I haven't had a helicopter explode under me and the wreckage pin me to the ground. I haven't lost a whole crew…I'm sorry, I don't mean to bring up the loss of your crew, but the fact that you were able to recover and continue serving your country…that's strength." Cece squeezed her arm. "I hope I didn't overstep, but Claire told me about your crew last time I was here."

Nic cocked a slight smile. "It's okay. It's not a secret." Nic picked at the label on the neck of her bottle.

"We all deal with battle stress and PTSD differently, and some of us don't deal with it at all and it ages us both physically and mentally. That optimistic kid who joined the Army at twenty-one isn't the same woman fifteen years later, sitting here."

"I get it, I really do."

"What can I do to help, Nic?"

Nic shook her head. "Nothing. This is work I have to do. I mean, I'm good, really. All told, I'm really fortunate to be here." She waved her hands. "I have a wife and family to come home to, who support me, so I have nothing to complain about. There are just times when it doesn't leave me and I just wondered how you deal with it."

Cece smiled at her. "I feel it when the weather changes." Clearly, she was trying to downplay it. "My shoulder aches with the change in weather."

Nic rubbed her face. "Oh, I get that. My face aches when it's cold."

"Is it hurting you now?" Cece smiled around the tip of the bottle.

"No, why?" Nic frowned. "Oh, I gotcha, 'cause it's 'killing you,' right? Cute, Sergeant."

Nic slapped at her, missing as Cece dodged the contact.

"Look, Nic, I'm no expert. All I can say is that this is how I deal with things. I put those feelings in a box, push the box back into the closet, and deal with them when I'm with my priest or in counseling. I have to be honest, I worry about this new job I'm starting. I'm still carrying a gun, but this time I'm dealing with students and families, so hopefully the stress level is way down here." Cece moved her hand inches above the deck. "But I don't know what might happen, so I've told myself that I'll get a counselor here when the time comes."

Nic smiled at Cece's frankness. She wanted to

tell her that she'd been going to a group for sufferers of PTSD, but she just couldn't. It wasn't that she was ashamed, it was more like it wasn't working for her. Some people liked to spill their guts, but she wasn't one of them.

"You never cease to amaze me, buddy." She tipped her bottle toward Cece, who tapped the neck with hers.

"I don't know how, but I appreciate it."

The door slid open. "Hey, you gals haven't touched the nibbles."

"Sorry, honey, we've just been catching up." Nic stood up and walked over to Claire. "Who is this little sleepy monster?" Nic kissed Grace's face and then nuzzled her neck, growling. Grace squealed and then grabbed Nic, pulling her closer for a kiss. "I'll take her, honey."

"Thanks." She handed Grace over, then whispered in Nic's ear. "She had a little scary dream."

Nic frowned and hugged Grace tighter. "How's my little bug doing?"

"Fine." Grace tucked her arms between them and laid her head on Nic's shoulder.

"Cece brought you a gift."

Grace's head popped off Nic's shoulder. "Hi, Cece."

Nic walked over and sat down.

"I did. I think your mom has it in the house. Want me to get it?"

Grace nodded and lay back on Nic's shoulder.

"Did you have a good nap?" Nic knew the answer but wanted Grace to tell her what happened. Grace gently shook her head.

"What happened?"

Grace lifted her head to whisper into Nic's ear. "Someone came to take you away."

"What?"

Grace nodded again, then slipped two fingers into her mouth, a comfort sign she reverted to when she was scared.

"Who came to take me away?"

"A bad man."

"Hmm. You know I'm not going anywhere, right?"

"But Momma, he said he was going to take you back, away."

"Oh, sweetie. I'm not going anywhere. I'm right here giving you big hugs." Nic tried her best to dismiss Grace's fears, but Nic knew it would take a little time to purge the nightmares that seemed to plague them all. When she'd first come home, Grace had a hard time looking at Nic. An eye patch and a swollen face with stitches didn't help. Though Grace had run to Nic as she worked her way through the airport crowd, she shied away as Nic bent to pick her up and didn't warm up to her for days. Nic hated to admit that she was the monster that plagued Grace's nightmares for a while until she got used to her momma again.

"Here you go, kiddo." Cece knelt down and smiled at Grace. "I hope you like him."

Grace hugged the bear to her chest. "Thank you, Cece."

Cece tousled her hair. "You are most welcome, little one."

"Where is your daughter?"

"Oh, Melita is home with her grandma. She can't come yet."

"Why?"

Nic spoke before Cece. "Honey, Cece is living in

a hotel right now, so there isn't anyone to take care of Melita."

"We could take care of Melita." Grace rolled her eyes and said matter-of-factly, "I have enough toys for her if she needs toys to play with. Really!" Grace's face lit up. She'd been begging for a little sister and this was almost as good in her eyes, Nic was sure.

Nic and Cece both chuckled at the expression on Grace's face.

"Well, I appreciate you sharing your toys. As soon as I get a place, I promise to bring Melita over and you girls can play together."

"Okay. Momma, can I have a cracker?"

"Of course you can, sweetie." Nic pulled a plate and filled it with a few nibbles. "Here you go. Help yourself, Cece." Nic pointed to the food. "Wonder where Claire is."

⁂

Claire looked out at Nic and Cece on the deck. She'd wanted to go outside and sit with the gals, but she'd seen Nic looking serious as she talked to Cece. She wondered what they were talking about but sensed it was probably shop talk. Grace had finally walked out of her room, signaling nap time was over. Lucky for her, so was the prep for the barbeque.

"Okay, my part of this production is over. Your turn, honey." Claire held the platter toward Nic. "Switch?"

"Guess I'm up to bat now. How do you like your steak, Cece?" Nic grabbed the steak and shouldered Grace over to Claire.

"Medium. No blood."

"You got it."

Claire sat in Nic's seat. "Darn, I forgot my wine. Honey, do you mind?"

"No problem. Cece, want another beer?"

"Sure."

Claire swiveled toward Cece. "So, how was the police academy?"

"Good. The physical stuff was easy. The procedural stuff, that took a little more time to get down."

"I bet." Claire brushed Grace's hair to the side and kissed the top of her head. "I guess all the military training came in handy, huh?"

"Sorta. I was kinda surprised when some of the younger cadets washed out. Guess it's not like playing their video games."

"Here you go, buddy." Nic handed Cece her beer, then turned to Claire and kissed her before handing her the glass of wine. "Honey, did you want me to grill the veggies, too?"

"Sure you can handle all of that?" she said playfully.

"I'll show you what I can—"

"Honey, company."

Nic looked at Cece, her face heated. "Sorry."

Claire slapped at Nic's hand. "Silly."

Usually their playful banter was limited to just them, but every once in a while, Claire had to remind Nic that they weren't alone. Mostly Nic did it when Claire's best friend Jordan was around. She liked to try to embarrass Jordan, but Jordan gave as good as she got, and many a time Nic was the one with a red face.

"So, anyone special?"

"Claire..." Nic said.

"What? I'm just making conversation with Cece."

"It's okay. No, I'm not really looking to start anything right now. I need to focus on the new job and getting a home ready so Lita can move up here with me."

"I bet she was excited to have you home."

"I'm not sure. I wasn't exactly home a lot before I left for the academy. I mean I got to come home a couple of weekends, but the police academy is pretty intense."

"I bet."

"So, what have you been up to, Claire?"

"Me? Well, I started back to school, finally. You'll probably see me on campus sometimes. I started the teaching program."

"That's great." Cece settled back into her seat. It was obvious to Claire that she didn't like talking about her personal life. It had taken Nic a long time to open up to her as well, so she figured it was the way of these military women and didn't take it personally when Cece changed the subject.

"Yeah. In fact, I'm taking Grace to the Women's March next weekend with a bunch of my fellow teaching students. We're exercising our ability to question authority. Want to come?"

Cece looked over her head toward Nic. Claire turned around just in time to see Nic shaking her head.

"Hey, if you won't go with me, honey, maybe I can get Cece to escort Grace and me." Claire turned back to Cece. "What do you think? Wanna join us?"

"Women's March, next weekend, huh? Let me check my work schedule." Cece pulled out her phone and scrolled through it. "It looks like I have to work that weekend."

"Hmm, likely story. That's okay, I'm going with

a bunch of women from school. I'm in a diversity club and we're all knitting pink hats for the event. Maybe I can knit you and Nic one, too. You gals can wear them in solidarity that day, even if you can't be there."

"Uh…" Cece's head bobbed in agreement. "I'm not sure the department will let me wear it to work, but I'll be with you in spirit, Claire."

"How about you, honey? Will you wear one?"

"Can I be frank? Hell, no. I am not putting on a hat that is supposed to resemble a—"

"Nicole." Claire covered Grace's ears.

"Sorry." Nic clasped her hand over her mouth and started laughing.

Grace pulled at Claire's hands. "What did Momma say?"

"Nothing, sweetie. She was just trying to be funny."

"So, you're taking Grace to the Women's March?" Cece asked.

"I think she's old enough to learn that as a woman she has a right to stand up for herself." Claire stiffened.

She and Nic had a long talk about whether Grace was old enough. Nic came down on the side of caution, while Claire had thought it was a good idea to expose Grace to civil disobedience. The fight had started when Nic had literally put her foot down and questioned the soundness of Claire's decision. It was one of the few times they had argued about parenting choices. The fact that Nic would even question Claire's decision irritated her. Perhaps it had been the condescending way Nic had referred to the women as "nutjobs." Maybe it had been the outrageous images Nic had made a point to print out and stick on her mirror with the question, "Does this look like a place for a child?"

Claire had to admit that some of the images weren't flattering, but Claire was outraged at the current political climate and wasn't about to be silenced, especially by her own wife. Now it was a matter of principle. When she told some of her friends at school, they all agreed that Claire needed to bring Grace and take a stand. Grace was her daughter, and she had no intention of being confrontational. She just wanted this to be something Grace remembered when she was older.

"I agree." Cece smiled. "Where is the march happening? On the campus?"

"No, down in Monterey."

"Hmm." Cece nodded rather uncomfortably.

"Steaks are almost done. Grace, why don't you tell Cece what grade you're in while Mommy helps me with the food. Mommy?"

"Sure, sweetheart." Claire shifted Grace. "I'll be right back. Fresh beer." She bit her tongue as she got up. Oh, Nic was going to catch hell. She knew when Nic was giving her the "that's enough" signal. She followed Nic and barely contained her sarcasm when she said, "Right behind you, sweetheart."

Chapter Four

elcome, Officer Ramirez. I'm glad to have a fellow top in the department." A "top," or first shirt, was usually a reference to a first sergeant or the top of a company's enlisted ranks. It didn't quite mesh with the bars on Lieutenant Murdoch's collar. He looked more like a student than a lieutenant in the University Police Department. Then again, most of the officers she'd seen so far were a cross between clean-cut frat boy and beach lovin' surfer dude. How he knew she was former Army surprised her, but that he knew her rank meant he'd gotten access to her file. She'd need to remember that moving forward in the department. While lots of departments had watercooler gossip, personnel information was usually confidential.

"Thank you, sir. I'm glad to be here." She offered a firm handshake and a starched appearance for her first day at work.

"You can drop the 'sir.' See combat?"

"Sir?" That wasn't usually the first question she got when meeting someone for the first time, but it was usually in the mix eventually when someone found out she'd been enlisted.

"I saw your jacket. Said you were retired Army."

"Yes, sir."

"Medical discharge?"

Her back stiffened, pulling the creases of her uniform to razor-sharp peaks. Suddenly, she didn't like where this line of questioning was going.

"No. But if you're asking me if I'm fit for duty, sir, let me assure you I passed my physical agility test without issue, my psych eval and the post certification with flying colors. I humped an M4 through Afghanistan and survived five tours of duty there."

Murdoch put his hands up. "Whoa, Ramirez. Just making some conversation with a new officer on my shift. Calm down,"

She knew how to respect the rank, but as for the person under the bar…well, he would have to earn her trust, and he wasn't doing a very good job of it so far. She was surprised he wasn't clutching his head from the hole she was boring through it with her eyes. She'd established the "no bullshit" stare during her first two tours in Afghanistan. The last three were just refinement exercises to get the laser stare perfected. Her squad knew enough to cut her a wide berth and do their jobs. It was clear she'd have to break in a whole new crew, because they definitely weren't going to break her.

Not this time.

Murdoch looked at his watch, perhaps an attempt to break the tension in the office.

"What are you still doing here, Lieutenant?" A distinguished man with stars on his collar indicating the rank of chief tossed a file on the conference table and made his way to the smell of coffee. "Jesus, this stuff looks like it was made yesterday." He swirled the contents and held it at eye level watching the dark liquid swish around the pot. Clearly happy with the agitation, he drained the pot into his stainless steel mug. He added three packets of sweetener and enough half-and-half to make it palatable yet give him the necessary caffeine she was sure he was going to need for the rest of the day.

"How are you settling in, Ramirez?" He took a swig, then grimaced. "Christ, Murdoch. Make some new coffee." Without missing a beat, he tapped the lid on the wicked brew. "Glad you decided to come over here instead of the rent-a-cop outfit the feds hire over there on the installation. Their coffee is worse than ours."

"Thank you, sir." Ramirez jerked as he slapped her firmly on the shoulder.

"Well, I get to sample some of that sludge the feds call coffee. I'm off to a mutual aid meeting with the other chiefs in the county. Murdoch, what the hell are you doing still standing here? Get the hell out there and give Ramirez the nickel tour."

"Yes, sir," he said gruffly, clearly pissed at something.

"Call me if anything major pops up and leave the students alone. Especially the females. You feel me?"

"Yes, sir."

She noticed Murdoch held the door open and nodded for her to go out. "Let's go, Ramirez."

Before she hit the door, he held up his hand, stopping her. "Your jacket. It's gonna be cold later." She looked out at the blue skies and then back at him, puzzled. "You're not from around here are you?"

"LA"

"Ah, well, welcome to Monterey, where the liquid sunshine comes in around three o'clock. You can set your watch by it." He pointed to the dark fog bank rolling in past the highway as they rounded the corner to the vehicle parking lot.

Monterey was nothing like LA, and she was

glad for that. While she would miss her family, she wanted someplace safe for her daughter to grow up, and that meant getting out of the neighborhood she'd grown up in and out of. Joining the military wasn't just something to do while she figured out her life. It had a purpose: to get her out without having to explain to her family why. Her brother Santino had joined a gang and it had broken her mother's heart, but her mom didn't understand he'd done it mostly out of survival. Cece knew he liked the brotherhood it offered to a skinny kid with only a sister as his immediate family. Cousins abounded throughout the neighborhood, but Santino was much older and looked up to. He had a reputation, a well-deserved one, that gave him the adoration of the large brood.

Well, Cece didn't need that kind of admiration. All she wanted was to raise her daughter in a safe environment away from guns, gangs, and the urban guerilla warfare that was taking place in the inner city of Los Angeles.

"So, Ramirez, what brought you to CSUMB?"

"A job."

"No kidding." Murdoch flashed her a toothy grin as he adjusted his belt before sitting in the driver's seat of the cruiser. "What made you get out of the Army?"

"It was my time to retire and I didn't want to do another tour overseas." Cece settled into her seat and suddenly regretted putting on the jacket. The tight confines, the laptop in the center, the shotgun rack, and the overall cramped space gave a feeling of claustrophobia.

"Third infantry myself. I loved it over there. Well, except the sand spiders. Those bastards scared the shit out of me." Murdoch eased out onto the street and toward the center of campus.

Cece took her time getting to know someone. She didn't spill her guts to the first interested person, curious co-workers—hell, it took her time to open up to someone she was dating. She'd let him try as he might, but she wasn't about to open up to Murdoch.

"Let's take a drive through campus housing. It'll give you the lay of the land since a majority of our calls come from out there and the dorms." He flipped his lights on, cranked on the wheel, and did a U-turn in the middle of the street, disregarding the oncoming traffic. Students walked along the street, a few flipping the bird while others were hypnotized by their phones. A few girls in yoga pants sprinted down the street. Murdoch watched the action, and when they'd passed the girls he followed their progress in the rearview mirror.

"Hey, eyes on the road, Lieutenant." She pushed against the dash as he slammed on the brakes, barely stopping before hitting a kid riding his skateboard across the street.

"Jaywalking motherfucker." He rolled his window down. "Hey, crosswalk man." Another obscene gesture was his reward for the admonishment. "Damn students. One of these days one of these little entitled bastards is going to get themselves killed if they don't pay attention."

The kid weaved his way around pedestrians and then flip-kicked the board up and onto the sidewalk. Skills. She had to hand it to the kid, he had mad skills. Cece gave Murdoch a sideways glance and shook her head

"What?"

She was starting to understand why the chief told

Murdoch to leave the students alone. Nothing worse than a man with a badge and an attitude to use it.

"Nothing, sir." Cece looked out at the rugged landscape passing on her right. What had she gotten herself into?

꧁꧂

Cece stepped away from the apartment and the woman ranting about the noise coming from downstairs. She figured Murdoch could handle the overly excitable woman. She noted the address and made a few notes before tucking her pad in her cargos. The off-campus housing wasn't really off campus, she had learned in her short time on the job, it was just the old military housing that had been gifted to the university when they closed Fort Ord. It lay about three miles east of the main part of campus. The bigger issues had come when they bisected the base, carving parts out for the local city, CSUMB, University of Santa Cruz, City of Monterey, City of Seaside, and the military, which still had servicemembers housed on what was left of the now-annexed base. Cronies of several senators had gotten access to some of the property at fire-sale prices and made a killing off their "investment." All aboveboard, she was sure. Right. Guns into plowshares or some crock, if she remembered all of the dust-up around closing a military base the size of Fort Ord and turning it into a university.

Well, that university was now her employer, so who was she to judge? Once she finished the academy, she was a free agent. No one had paid for her college, except the pound of flesh she'd left behind in exchange for her GI Bill, so she could pick and choose where she wanted to go. Being a woman of color who was fluent in both English and Spanish meant she was a hot commodity. Add that to her military background and discipline, and it was no surprise she'd had her share of offers.

"Yes, ma'am. You're right. You pay to be here, too. I understand," Murdoch said, backing away from the stairs. "I've spoken to the residents downstairs and they assured me that they're done for the night. If it gets loud again, you have our phone number."

Cece's phone vibrated in her pocket. Pulling it from her pocket, she walked to the car and covered her ear as she answered the phone.

"Hi, baby."

"Hi, Mommy."

"What are you doing? Where's abuela, Lita?"

"She's right here. I asked her if I could call you. I miss you, Mommy."

"I miss you, too, baby girl."

"When are you coming home?"

"Next week. I have a surprise for you, Melita." Cece walked farther away from the continuing commotion behind her, keeping an eye on Murdoch just in case he got into trouble.

"Ooh, Mommy. Is it a puppy? I want a puppy. I'm a big girl. I can take care of a puppy. Pulleeezzzzeeee."

"It's not a puppy, honey. We need to wait until we get our own place and then we can talk about a puppy, or maybe a kitty."

"Oh, a kitty, Mommy."

Melita's short attention span worked to Cece's benefit. As long as she could dangle something else in front of her daughter it would stop the whining for the moment. God, she missed her baby girl. Soon, she thought. Next week or two, she'd be moving her munchkin up the coast to the little townhouse Cece had managed to rent. She wasn't sure she was ready to buy in one of the hottest real estate markets in the country, but it wouldn't be a bad investment even if the job didn't work out. She hadn't used her VA loan yet, and being from California afforded her another loan possibility as a vet.

Decisions, decisions.

Time was on her side. Tucking the phone into her cargos, she studied the houses out at East Garrison. Functional, bland, and affordable. It looked like typical military housing. She'd seen it on a ton of bases. But, what more did students need? She'd been told that the housing made the college millions. They had assumed it from the military so they didn't have to invest in building it, which meant a veritable gold mine for the university. She'd been told that it was all put under the umbrella of a foundation and that the foundation gifted the university millions because of it. Her in-service had included statistics on crime, population, restrictions, and how they interfaced with local PDs. It had also been very clear on what to expect in the diverse housing arrangements, which included families as well as single college students. What a mix, she thought. The upside was that the college only had a few mixed streets now. They had learned from their earlier experiments that single students and students with families didn't quite work together.

Yep, policing on CSUMB was nothing like policing on a base. The radio transmitted another garbled call and they were off again, this time to a drunken brawl.

Well, maybe not so different.

Chapter Five

Nic leaned back, balancing on two of the four rickety metal chair legs. She couldn't stop looking at the body hanging off the huge crucifix that dominated the small room. For some reason the body seemed to be precariously close to the circle of chairs. Every meeting it was the same grouping, and every meeting Nic fixated on the huge cross with the too-realistic man, a crown of thorns dripping blood down his face. The constant reminder they were in the basement of a local church wasn't lost on Nic, either. The persecuted, the broken, the…Well, she'd had enough.

Tonight would be her last night for this group. She'd given it a couple of months, months spent listening to the same stories, seeing the same faces in tortured relief, and months of silence on her part.

"Colonel, would you like to share?"

Why did they always address her by her rank? She wasn't in uniform and she never introduced herself by her rank. Yeah, it was definitely time to exit stage right.

A hand tapped her shoulder lightly.

Nic searched the circle of empty eyes staring at her. Sure, they were wondering if she'd say anything tonight. She hated to disappoint them, but she did anyway.

"No thanks." She looked at the fresh-faced kid and

group leader, Rod White, who she was sure still looked like his high school senior picture. The only difference between the Rod of then and the Rod of today? The missing right arm and leg, and a mangled left hand that perched on the stick shift of the wheelchair. His cheery demeanor, while seeming like it stayed painted on, was always surprising to Nic. What did he have to be happy about?

Yeah, her pissy, cynical side had taken over and she didn't wish that on anyone. Her shrink had convinced her that going to "group" might help her open up, but it had the opposite effect. She relived every jarring moment of the bombing each time she attended. It was hard to forget the reason she was going at all.

"Well, when you're ready, we'll be here, Colonel."

Embarrassed, Nic didn't have the heart to tell him she needed to bail on the group. Like an earworm but not a song, she thought about bailing for the third time in just the last two minutes. She knew her shrink had a name for her avoiding group, but she would just call it a Freudian thing. She nodded and avoided everyone's stare, and instead looked over at the same stack of store-bought cookies and punch that seemed to never get eaten or drunk no matter how many people visited the table, all laid out on the table in the same fashion every time they met. Was there some handbook for church groups that dictated what would be served and how it was to be put on the table?

Nic pulled at the collar of her button-down shirt, trying to dislodge it from the sweat that coated her body. The suffocating heat of the room had that sickening sugary smell wafting through it. Nic would never be able to eat another supermarket sugar cookie as long as she lived without thinking of the church basement and Jesus hanging over the group.

A man cleared his throat.

Great. Mr. Overshare was ramping up to start his usual routine. Eyes rolled, and a few huffed then extracted themselves from their chairs and gorged on cookies. She was certain it was to keep their mouths busy so they wouldn't say something hostile, which wasn't allowed.

"Everyone gets to be heard in group," Roy had informed Nic on her first night.

Nic joined the chorus of rolled eyes.

Yep. That was group.

❧ ❧ ❧

"Colonel, you okay?"

Nic closed her eyes and pasted on a slight smile. "I'm good, Rod. How are you doing?"

His head bobbed up and down. "I'm good. I just found out my girlfriend is pregnant and so…yeah. I'm gonna be a dad."

"Congrats. That's great news." One didn't have to be a mind reader to decipher the mix of emotions flitting across his face. "Freaking out a little, huh?"

"I'm not sure how it happened, but I think I'm pretty excited."

"Wait, you don't know how it happens? I'm not an expert on such matters, but even I know how babies are made." Nic offered him a cup of the sugary mixture they were calling punch.

He waved it off and pointed to his mug with a straw that had the end pinched. "Thanks, I bring my own hooch."

"Is that spiked? You sure you should be driving?"

While she was pretty sure he knew she was kidding, she never put it past anyone anymore.

"Funny, Colonel." Rod looked around the room and then leaned toward Nic. "Can I speak to you after group, Colonel?"

Nic got a funny feeling in her stomach. She glanced around the room the same way Rod had and, feeling a tad suspicious, wondered why he wanted to speak with her.

"Um…"

"I would really appreciate it." His eyes softened. He looked like he was almost going to cry.

"Sure, Rod. I've got time." She patted him on the shoulder. "We better get back or Tank is going to start telling that same ol' story again."

"Christ, I wish he would—"

Nic looked back at Rod, who clamped his mouth shut.

"Sorry."

"No, it's good to know I'm not the only one thinking that way."

"It's not him, it's me. Guess I'm just a little over-whelmed," he said, rolling past Nic. "Okay everyone, let's finish up."

Nic wondered why Rod was pressing her to talk to him. Guess she'd find out in thirteen minutes and counting.

❧❧❧❧

A plate of cookies and a full gallon of punch still sat on the table. An offering of sorts to the cleanup gods, Nic thought as she sat in the single chair opposite Rod. While the room had finally emptied of its inhabitants, the heat was still oppressive. Maybe Nic should have told Rod to meet her upstairs where the crisp night air could work its magic.

Rod wheeled himself in front of Nic and cleared his throat.

"Colonel…" He lifted a crooked finger up to his neck and pulled at the collar of his shirt.

"It's always so damn hot in here."

"Maybe it's penance for our sins." Rod cast a weary look up at the large savior hanging off the wall. "Don't look so surprised, Colonel. I might be the group leader, sorta, but I'm not immune to those kinda thoughts." He shook his head. "Sometimes I think I'm just an imposter sitting here coaxing people to share their grief, their loss, and their experiences. That somehow they'll find out and kick me out of group."

Nic wasn't big on self-pity and she especially hated it on herself, but she could relate to the young man in a lot of ways. It was what bound most survivors together, the loss, the insurmountable grief, and the wondering if they would ever be normal again. She, too, had to recognize that this was her new normal.

Nic pulled a deep breath. She wanted to go home and be released from this whole idea of group. "So, what did you want to talk to me about, Rod?"

"Well, you probably could guess that I have a lot of respect for you, Colonel. I mean not just for your rank, though you've earned that, but I mean as a person. You're very reserved and thoughtful in group, and I appreciate your being here. I think it has a calming effect on everyone."

Nic knew Rod was slinging a line of bullshit, but she wondered why. She wasn't his commanding officer. She didn't have anything to do with his world, whether it spun clockwise or went skidding off its axis. She ran her thumbnail under another fingernail and cleaned it.

"Rod, look, I'm a straight shooter so I'm just going to say this, and I hope you don't get pissed, but what a load of horseshit. You barely know me. I mean, yeah, I've been coming to group all of about three months, but I gotta be honest with you, I decided tonight was my last night. I just can't do it anymore." She looked over at him. He leaned toward her, smiling that smile that was clearly his stock-in-trade.

"I can appreciate that you might not believe me, Colonel. I mean, we've only talked a few times after group, but I've appreciated your gentle way of expressing yourself."

Gentle. That was a descriptor Nic hadn't heard before.

"I don't have any family around here and my folks aren't young and are having a hard time dealing with all of this." He swept his damaged hand down his body. "My dad is a hard-core military man. He never shows weakness, thinks it's a sign of being soft. So, you can imagine what he said when he saw me. 'Son, you're gonna walk again, hear me?' He just doesn't understand and accept this is my new normal."

Acceptance.

Nic was familiar with a father who didn't accept what was in front of him. Her own father had turned his back on her when she'd come out as a lesbian. He still shunned her the few times she'd gone home to visit her mother. It had been harder for her to accept his unwillingness to embrace her and her lifestyle. Indeed, Nic knew a lot about a father who couldn't come to terms with a child and who they were.

"What can I do to help, Rod?"

Chapter Six

The crowd around Claire was electric, the energy palpable. In front of her, throngs of women and a smattering of men held signs high above their heads.

Equality for all.

Our ovaries, Our decision.

Grab this, with a picture of a hand flipping the bird.

Some were so vulgar even Claire blushed at the double meanings. As long as a fight didn't break out with the demonstrators that were baiting them, she'd stay. The moment things went south, so would she. She didn't want to give Nic any ammunition to say she was right about not bringing Grace.

Behind her the crowd slimmed some, but they were just as enthusiastic. She was glad she'd slathered Grace in sunscreen with the sun screaming down on them. A welcome relief, considering some of those participating in women's marches throughout the world would be battling not just the crowds, but cold, foggy weather.

"Dump Trump," someone chanted as the crowd echoed.

Claire stood in the middle of a group of fellow students from classes at CSUMB. Many of the women wore pink hats symbolizing their sorority of sisterhood. While she felt like one of them, she just couldn't bring herself to wear one, even after she'd knitted one and tried it on. She also wasn't going to put one on Grace, who was already asking questions about the colorful display. She hated it when Nic was right, so she just wouldn't tell her.

"Mommy, mommy, mommy." Grace's outstretched arms indicated her immediate need. Claire grunted. The princess wasn't a sack of flour anymore, more like a sack of potatoes. Now at seven years old, Grace needed to be broken of the need to be carried.

"Isn't this exciting?" Maryann practically glowed with excitement. Claire, ten to twenty years older than most of her fellow students, wasn't quite as enthusiastic, but she knew she needed to be here. To be silent was to be complicit, and there was no way she was giving her stamp of approval to this administration.

Claire smiled. "Exciting."

"Hey, where's Nic?" Maryann pumped her sign up and down as the crowd moved slowly down the street.

Before she could answer, Maryann screamed, "Selfie." In an instant they were surrounded by chanting women who suddenly stopped to smile at the camera a few feet above them.

"Hey, text me that."

"Yeah, me, too. I want to send it to my mom."

"I'm going to post it and tag you on social media, so all of you can get it from there," Maryann said, mindlessly walking as she gazed down at her screen posting it to all her social media sites.

"So, where's Nic?" Maryanne said without looking at Claire.

"Home."

"Bummer. Too bad she didn't come and see all of

this girl power."

Though Claire had tried to convince Nic to join the protest, she knew crowds weren't in Nic's wheelhouse at the moment. However, she wouldn't give up trying to get her out of the house.

"You know, sweetheart, you look fine." Claire cupped Nic's face and pulled her in for a kiss.

Nic reached down and pulled Claire closer to her, their bodies molding together. This, this closeness, is what Claire had missed most while Nic was gone. Without thinking, she wrapped her arms around Nic's neck, wove her hands through Nick's hair. It was longer than usual, but Claire wasn't complaining. She'd take a long-haired shaggy Nic at home any day. The alternative wasn't something she wanted to think about.

Pulling back, she looked up at her lover, her thumbs running over Nic's lips. She studied Nic's face. If one didn't know, they would never have guessed that less than a year ago Nic was lying in a hospital bed and with a broken orbital socket, fractured cheekbone, broken ribs, a broken wrist, missing teeth, and a severe concussion that still plagued her today. Her orbital surgery has saved her sight, and Nic was nearing the end of a lengthy process of receiving dental implants to make her smile picture perfect.

"How is your headache?"

Nic flashed that mischievous smile that often got her into trouble, but Claire knew this time it was only a smile. The PTSD had taken its toll on their relationship and lately Nic had pulled away from Claire emotionally. Her early weeks at home had been a whirlwind of activity, doctor's visits, therapy, and long bouts of "quiet reflection," as coined by the therapist Nic was seeing. They'd gone to therapy together at first. However, it had become clear that Nic needed to deal with her demons without Claire present. She suspected it was because Nic didn't want her to hear all the gory details. The truth, Claire knew, was that Nic was private when it came to her foibles. While Claire didn't see Nic's injuries as a weakness, that wasn't how Nic saw them.

Outside, Nic was mostly Nic. Her scars were a roadmap of her life in the military. The lower scar on her back, where the exhaust manifold of the helicopter had trapped her to the ground, was rough and long, the remnant of the helicopter crash on her first deployment to Iraq. It was fading as much as it could, and Claire wished the memory of that accident would fade, too. Nic had been the only survivor of that tragic accident in Iraq, her whole crew lost. Scars on Nic's face from her more recent accident gave Nic that ruggedly handsome look. At least, that was how Claire saw it.

Inside, Nic was less Nic. The internal scars were harder to see, but not less evident. Her carefree love of life had turned into something more like survival mode. Nic constantly looked over her shoulder the few times they had gone out together, and she was constantly on alert. Their first date night had Nic positioning her back against the wall, facing the door. She was engaged in the conversation, but Claire couldn't help but notice Nic's gaze darting toward the door each time it opened. Her body tensed and then relaxed as the guests entered the restaurant. If she assessed them as families she ignored them, but if she felt something was wrong she couldn't take her eyes off them. This was the new Nic Caldwell. Nic referred to herself as a sheepdog now—always on patrol. She couldn't shake the image of Nic walking the fence line, her tail wagging expectantly. If humor couldn't get them through the adjustments, nothing would.

"Ma'am, I see you've brought your daughter to the March. Can you tell us what today means to you?"

Caught daydreaming about her lover, Claire looked at the reporter.

The woman held a microphone with a KSLT logo on it, or K-SLUT as it was referred to by some in the community who hadn't missed the fact that the women on the conservative station were always young and perky, and the men were aging wannabe Hannity types. Claire didn't recognize the reporter.

She pulled Grace closer and studied the young woman offering a smile, and politely replied, "I'm sure I don't have to tell you what this means to thousands of women today who are marching all over this world. I mean, look around at all the signs. We're marching for equality, marching to stopping abuse, and focus a magnifying glass on the issue. We're here to raise our voices and give voice to those who can't, or for those who don't feel comfortable speaking."

"Well, I mean that's kind of obvious, right?" The reporter pushed her boxy glasses up her nose.

"Oh, hey, everyone. Claire's on the news." Maryanne threaded her arm through Claire's and pulled her closer.

"Oh, is this your partner?"

"What?" Claire looked at Maryanne. "No, we're classmates at CSUMB." Claire gently pulled her arm out of Maryann's clutches.

"So, what do you think of the women's march?"

The microphone was shoved at Maryanne, who seemed to welcome its closeness to her mouth. Maryanne even moved closer to the mic, if that was possible, practically eating the foam head. "This is fantastic. All of these women, and men, marching for what's right, what's fair. Equity," Maryanne yelled and pumped her fist into the air. The crowd behind her echoed her cry.

"Is this a political statement or—"

"Fuck yeah, it's a political statement. We want that cheese puff in the white house out," someone behind Claire yelled.

Claire pulled Grace's head to her shoulder and muffled her ears before she addressed the reporter.

"We aren't going to sit by and watch while our voices are minimized. We want the respect we are due. We want to show people that women aren't second-class citizens and have the right to be heard. Our voices together, our unity, means we aren't pussies to be grabbed, things to be objectified or look pretty on your arm. Or that we aren't just baby-making machines needed to propagate this new world order. We have fought for our place at the table and we aren't going to sit back and watch as some man, who has little respect for women, decides we don't belong at the table, or that our reproductive rights should be decided by those with testicles, or dictates who we marry and who should serve our country."

Claire stopped herself before she said something that could hurt Nic's career. It wasn't a secret that many wives avoided marches and rallies for fear their husbands would pay the price for their outspokenness. Couple that with being one of the few lesbian couples at NPS and it was a recipe for disaster. She wanted Nic to keep that teaching job at the Naval Postgraduate School. Desperately.

It was a delicate balance between the military and a person's personal life. She lived it every day. Her mind was always hypervigilant about who she talked to and what she said. She'd once ran into General Stoddard's wife in the commissary. She saw Grace and immediately came over and patted her head.

"What a beautiful little girl." She bent down, gently pinched Grace's cheek, and smiled. "What's your name?"

Grace looked at Claire and then the floor.

"It's okay, sweetie. I'm General Stoddard's wife, Millie."

"Mrs. Stoddard, it's a pleasure to meet you." Claire smiled. "Honey, you can tell Mrs. Stoddard your name. We had a Stranger Danger class recently, and on top of that Grace is shy, too."

"Aw, what a beautiful child. Well, you don't have to worry about me, Grace. I have children, too." She patted Grace's hand reassuringly.

"Do you have a wife, too?" Grace asked innocently.

Flummoxed was the only word that came to mind as Claire watched Millie stumble over her words and then gain her composure. It was two seconds, tops, before the wifely façade dropped into place.

"Why, well no. I mean not that there is anything wrong with having two moms. I mean, I have a husband."

"Why don't you have a wife? My mommy does." The innocent words of a child, spoken in honesty and without a malicious thought, seemed to throw Millie for a split-second, again.

"You're a lucky daughter to have two mommies who love you, Grace." Millie was the consummate company wife. Nothing ever flustered them. They didn't overreact when presented with something different, and they were very children friendly.

"I'm sorry—" Claire started to continue but was stopped.

"It's fine. She's not making me uncomfortable, if that's what you're thinking. I have a daughter who's been with her partner for twelve years, and we are thrilled she's found someone so loving and caring. We love her wife as if she were our own and they have given us our only grandchildren. Our sons are too busy living *la vida loca*, or something like that." She chuckled and snapped her fingers. "I hope I haven't made you uncomfortable, Claire." She patted Claire's shoulder reassuringly. "I know some people get goosed up when they see me. I wasn't born into this life, but I definitely know how the wives are around here. Would you like to come for tea sometime? I do a little tea once a month, and I would love for you and Grace to join us."

"Oh, you don't have to do that." Suddenly it was Claire who felt uncomfortable.

"I know I don't have to, but I'd like to have you and your charming daughter over."

"I have to warn you, she isn't always this charming." Claire looked down at Grace and gently pulled at the stray ends of hair, tucking them behind her ears.

"I've had children, I know they can be monsters sometimes, but I'm okay with it if you are. Please say yes."

Who denied the General's wife? When she asked, you said yes. Automatically.

"Of course, I would love to come to tea. Please let me know what I can bring."

Millie leaned in. "Have any trashy novels you'd

like to share with the group?"

Surprised, Claire pulled back. "Um, yes, but—"

"Good, we like to call it book club so our husbands—and wives, now—think we are doing something literary."

Millie pulled out a business card with her information and slipped it into Claire's hand. "Next week, Wednesday, at eleven. Don't forget your book. Bye, Grace. I'll see you soon." She took the liberty of kissing the girl's forehead before waving to Claire.

Claire watched as the woman pushed her cart down the right-hand side of the aisle—the military way to shop the commissary—and turned the corner.

That had been two weeks ago, and now Claire felt a presence at her side. She turned and found Millie standing beside her, pink hat firmly ensconced on her head and holding a sign that had a uterus giving the finger. Suddenly, she didn't feel like she needed to worry about being outspoken, not if she was standing shoulder-to-shoulder with the General's wife.

"Who likes cheese doodles anyway?" Millie smiled and pumped her sign up and down.

"The White House is our house, and it's time to clean house! The White House is our house, and it's time to clean house!" The chant rose from behind them.

"You look familiar." The reporter looked at Millie and shoved the mic in her face. "Aren't you General Stoddard's wife?"

Millie's smile exploded as she regarded the reporter. "Why, yes, I am. I'm Millie Stoddard. Are you that conservative reporter from public TV? I've seen your show before. You're just here to bait these women, aren't you?"

"Are you afraid of the image you're sending to the wives of troops who are serving?" The reporter smirked after asking the question. She nodded to the cameraman to move in tighter on Millie.

"I've been a loyal supporter of our troops and have worked hard to make sure children have the support they need when their parents are overseas. I'll have you know, I marched for the ERA, I burned my bra. I might have been a teenager, but I've always been about my fellow wives and sisters. Does that surprise you? I won't pretend that I'm not conflicted by what's passing as leadership lately, but my heart and soul will always be with the troops and their families. Besides, my husband is the person serving. You don't see any rank on my collar, do you?"

"If memory serves me, the ERA couldn't even get ratified."

"I can assure you it wasn't from a lack of trying. Perhaps you should take a history lesson, young lady. The early suffragettes, who were beaten, raped, and practically killed just so you could have the right to vote and act like this, would be appalled at your attitude."

"Well, it just seems that…" She looked around at the growing crowd around them. "I mean let's be honest, Mrs. Stoddard. The military deserves the respect of the public and you being out here is so—"

"So what? Beneath me?"

"Well, you said it, I didn't."

"I'm proud of the military and the advances we've made. We are one of the biggest and most diverse organizations. We have women serving at the highest ranks. We have welcomed our LGBT troops with open arms, and we are working together to keep families strong while their loved ones serve overseas, most in combat areas. What the heck have you done? Claire's wife was wounded twice overseas, and she's getting ready to serve her country again as an instructor at the Naval Postgraduate School. Why don't you do more stories on those families?"

"Mrs. Stoddard, I'm sure I don't have to tell you. This…" She twirled in a circle motioning to the crowd around her. "This is the hottest story right now."

Millie just clucked her disapproval, dismissed the woman, and leaned over to say something to Grace, leaving Claire face-to-face with the reporter. Claire had to admire Millie for not letting the woman get under her skin too much. If only she'd learn that lesson a time or two.

"So, you're gay."

"I'm a lesbian, yes."

"Your wife is in the military. What does she think about you being out here and protesting the president?"

"She serves her commander-in-chief like any other officer or enlisted person in the military."

"Even if he is rescinding things like flying the Pride flag during Pride month at the Pentagon, or kicking out trans servicemembers?"

"Those are policies, and she doesn't make policy. Perhaps you should talk to our congressman Senator James. He voted with the president to change those policies."

"Why, when I can talk to you? You're on the front lines of attack from this administration. You have to live those policies every day. So why don't you give our audience an insight into what it's like to face the possible loss of benefits and privileges, like housing, medical care, maybe even your wife's retirement benefits and survivor benefits?"

"You're just being ridiculous now, trying to get me to react to your dog whistle. I'm not going to bite, so maybe you should move on to someone who's more easily manipulated by your comments. I don't think you'll have to go far to find someone." Claire pointed to a scuffle that had broken out between marchers and the police. "Look."

The reporter was almost drooling as she focused on the skirmish "John, let's go." The reporter practically pushed women out of her way to get to the scuffle. "Get a tight shot of those two women."

Chapter Seven

Nic scanned the small parking lot of the mini mart. The shopette was a favorite place of the local enlisted from base. It was within walking distance from the base, and had alcohol, cigarettes, and lottery tickets. What more could a young soldier need?

Nic double-checked the small list Claire had sent with her, crumbled it, and tossed it into the cup holder. She could remember four items. Jumping out of the car, she patted her back pockets for her phone and wallet.

Christ.

She could remember the four items and her wallet, but she needed a bungee cord for her phone. She'd left the damn thing at home, again. Shaking her head, she wondered what the hell they all did before technology replaced their minds.

Pushing through the doors, she spotted a couple of shaved tails laughing around the beer cooler. Pushing and shoving each other, they looked over their shoulders at Mrs. Patel, who was busy ringing someone up.

Nic caught sight of one of them stuffing a forty-ounce beer can inside his coat and then grabbing a case of beer. The other guy followed suit and shoved another forty in the waistband of his pants, draped his jacket over the bulge, and then adjusted his jacket to hide his waist. Shoplifting wasn't worth a dishonorable discharge, but some people had to learn the hard way.

Nic casually moved behind the guys as they took their place in line. As they placed the first case of beer on the counter, Nic heard Mrs. Patel greet them in her usual friendly way.

"Good afternoon, sir. Have a busy Friday night planned?" Her accent reminded Nic of the women she'd met while in Afghanistan. Pleasant, welcoming, and friendly.

"Yep, it's been a busy week and I'm ready to party. Right, Carl?" The soldier turned and high-fived his buddy behind him.

"Yep. I'm ready for some R and R, dude."

"Well, I hope you aren't drinking and driving."

"Oh, no, ma'am. We're just walking and drinking." He laughed, shelling out a few bucks.

"Are you gonna pay for that forty in your jacket, soldier?" Nic said, loud enough so that there was no mistake who, or what, she was referring to as she pointed to his jacket.

"I'm sorry, ma'am. I think you're confused."

"I'm not confused, son. It's not worth a dishon-orable for shoplifting."

His back straightened. He looked at Mrs. Patel and then back at Nic. His buddy put his beer on the counter and turned toward Nic, too.

"I think you're mistaken." He took a step toward Nic.

She sized him up. Skinny. No, scrawny was more like it. About her height. His buddy was a few inches shorter but built like a tractor. If his accent was any indication, he was from somewhere around Alabama.

"I don't make mistakes, son. So, here's a piece of advice: Pull that beer out of your jacket and either pay for it or leave it on the counter, and don't ever come back to this shop again."

"And if I don't?" He shouldered his buddy.

"I'll make sure you get drummed out of whatever branch you're in and do some heavy lifting for your bullshit."

"Who the fuck do you think you are, bitch?" He stepped closer and jumped in Nic's bubble. His fists clenched and raised to his chest.

"Don't add assaulting an officer to the charges, son." While Nic's words were calm and cool, her insides were vibrating. She didn't shrink from confrontation, and unfortunately this kid had more ego than brains, which was working against him at the moment. It was clear he was going to lose more than just his newly earned rank if he kept moving in the direction he was heading.

"You ain't my momma." His drawl was long and slow. Clearly, he hadn't heard Nic when she told him she was an officer.

Nic looked at Mrs. Patel. "Call the police."

"You gotta be kidding me." He pulled the forty out of his jacket and slammed it hard enough on the counter that the glass shattered, spraying everyone with beer.

"Give me your ID cards. You can have them back when I meet with your commanding officer."

"Fuck you. I ain't givin' you shit." He stepped back and Nic stepped forward.

Nic pointed to the camera behind the counter, causing him to look directly at it. "No worries. I'll just take that footage to the base police and run it to match your ID."

Suddenly, a young man jetted from behind the

swinging doors in the back with a baseball bat in his hands.

"You fucking Americans are all alike. You come in here and take what doesn't belong to you, thinking you can bully us into keeping quiet." The young man rushed toward them and Nic stepped in front of the two idiots.

"Benji," Mrs. Patel screamed. "Don't."

"Calm down, kid." Nic put her hands on his chest, trying to stop him.

A shooting pain traveled through her face as the kid's fist made contact with the left side of her jaw. Already amped on adrenaline, she growled, grabbed him by his T-shirt, and shoved him against the soda cooler. Shoving her face within inches of his, she lowered her voice. "You put your fucking hands on me again and I'll split that melon you call a head. You got me?" She heard the two soldiers behind her shuffling. Calling out over her shoulder, she said, "And you better stop right there, or you'll have more than one problem on your hands." She shot them a look as she held the kid on the tips of his toes.

"Oh, please, Miss Nic. Please don't hurt Benji."

"I'm not going to hurt him. Did you call the police?"

"I'm doing it right now. Right now. Please just put him down."

"Get your ass back to wherever you came from and get me a copy of the videotape of the last twenty minutes. Understand me?"

He nodded. "Don't come back out here until you have that copied for me."

Nic set him on his feet and unclenched her hands from his shirt.

"Now, for you two sorry excuses for soldiers." Nic stepped toward them with her hand out. "IDs. Now."

Nic looked at the broken counter and then back to Mrs. Patel. She shook her head. Assholes. A family just trying to make a living.

"What unit are you in?" Nic's hand was out, still waiting for their ID cards.

"Who the fuck do you think you are, dyke? We don't have to tell you jack," the brick shithouse said as he took a step toward her. When she didn't move, she caught his hands clenching into fists. His buddy stepped up behind him.

"Don't add assaulting a superior officer to the list of crimes you're going to be court-martialed over."

"You ain't no officer. What, for the gay army?"

Nic smiled. She'd dealt with the few whispers about her sexuality behind her back. Confrontation wasn't an issue for her, but assholes like this were. Reaching into her back pocket, she pulled out her wallet and jerked out her Military ID.

"That would be Colonel Dyke to you men."

Nic wanted to laugh as their faces melted with the news. Her ID showed proof of her rank and their stupidity.

"Let me give you some advice, gentlemen, and I use that term loosely. You represent the United States Military when you are out on the economy. As a representative, you need to be on your best behavior because you represent us all when you open those redneck mouths." The brick shithouse stiffened as his face contorted into a grimace. "I am not easily intimidated, but Mrs. Patel is when some shaved-tail assholes come into her shop and get caught stealing.

See, she's just trying to make a living. Aren't you Mrs. Patel?"

"Oh, yes, Miss Nic." She held the phone in her hand and didn't look at the men.

"So, you're taking food out of her family's mouths when you steal and you're presenting a really bad image of the US Military. The only solutions for this incident are either you give me your ID cards, or the police come and arrest you for theft, assault, and vandalism. They'll call your first sergeant or platoon leader and you'll be released into his or her care, then you'll face court-martial and probably charges in the civilian world, then your career is over." Nic snapped her fingers. She was getting impatient waiting. "A dishonorable discharge is just as bad as going to prison, boys. You'll never own firearms, not that I think you should considering your tempers, and your total lack of respect for different cultures, and you won't be able to get a job, either. Choice is up to you."

Neither soldier moved.

"Mrs. Patel?"

"Yes, Miss Nic?"

Nic nodded at the phone. "Please make that phone call."

Benji came out of the back room with a disc in his hand. "Here you are, Colonel."

"Thank you, Benji."

He'd calmed down considerably now and he bowed his head. "I'm sorry about earlier. It's just that this is my parents' store, this is all they have. They've worked so hard...I mean, you know. You've shopped here enough."

Nic patted the young man on the back. "I know, but you wouldn't be helping them if you went to jail, now would you?"

"No, of course not."

One of the guys groaned and whispered something about camels and intercourse.

She narrowed her eyes at the men. "You know that old saying when you're in too deep, stop digging? You need to shut up."

"Thanks, Benji." Nic waved the disc. "I appreciate your help."

Looking back at the two men, she put her hand out again. "It's either you two, me, and your commander, or the police. You decide."

The young man in the back whispered something to the brick shithouse. Fishing their IDs out of their wallets, they handed them over to Nic. She thought she heard one of them mumble, "Bitch."

"Unit, gentlemen?"

"Private First Class Sinclar. US Marine Corps, Charlie company attached to the POM, Presidio of Monterey."

Nic gave him a look when he didn't finish the sentence correctly. "Ma'am."

Nic looked at the other ID card. "What about you, Moffett? I'm sure your mother and father would be so proud of you right now, wouldn't they?"

"Ma'am, Private First Class Moffett, US Marine Corps, Charlie company attached to the POM."

Nic strummed the IDs across her fingers, walked around the men and assessed them. What a disappointment. "What language are you studying?" She prayed they didn't say—

"Arabic."

Great, so these yahoos would be deployed to a powder keg with their racist attitudes. Well, maybe she was wrong. Maybe they weren't racists, just bad at making decisions when it came to their shopping experiences.

"Who's your commanding officer?"

"Ma'am?" The skinny one paled.

"I don't speak Arabic well, but I can give it a try if that would help."

"No, ma'am."

"Good. Now who is your commanding officer?"

"Captain Goodwin, ma'am."

"Expect a phone call from Captain Goodwin tomorrow. Dismissed."

"Wait," one of them said, pointing to his ID in Nic's hand. "How are we supposed to get back on base?"

"Hmm, not my problem." Nic didn't feel sorry for the men, but she was pissed that they hadn't exhibited better social skills. "I'll see you tomorrow in Captain Goodwin's office." Grabbing the brick shithouse before he could leave, she turned him around.

"Did you pay for the damages?"

"Ma'am?"

"Mrs. Patel's counter and the beer bottle you shattered."

"I don't have that kind of money, ma'am."

"Well, I'm sure we can work out a payment plan to get this fixed, right Mrs. Patel?"

"Oh, it's no bother, Miss Nic." She waved her hands.

"Well, it's a bother to me, Mrs. Patel. We'll get this sorted."

"Are you forgetting something, gentlemen?"

She crossed her arms over her chest and stared them down.

"We apologize for the damages, Mrs. Patel."

Mrs. Patel nodded, but didn't say anything. Thankfully. Nic didn't want them thinking they were getting off with just an apology.

"Dismissed."

"What about our beers?"

"Really?"

"Yes, ma'am." The men ran once they were through the doors and jumped in their car.

"Oh, Miss Nic, I'm so sorry."

"Mrs. Patel what do you have to be sorry for? I'm the one that's sorry. They were assholes. I apologize on behalf of the Marine Corps, and we'll get this taken care of immediately." Nic lifted the disc. "Tell Benji thank you for the evidence. I appreciate it."

"I'm so sorry about Benji. He gets so steamed sometimes. You know?"

"I know, but he can't come running out here with a baseball bat. Next time they could have guns and he could get shot."

"I know. I've told him over and over again, but he's young and always ready to fight. I don't understand it."

"Is he your only child?"

"Yes, we could only have one. I'm blessed to have Benji."

"Well, he's young. Give him time."

"I hope you are right, Miss Nic."

"Okay, well I better pay for these and get home. Claire's going to wonder what happened to me."

"How is Miss Claire and Grace?"

"They're good."

"Such a lovely family you have."

"Thank you. I am blessed."

Walking out of the store, Nic realized she'd handled a confrontation without her PTSD flaring up. Maybe things were looking up.

⁕ ⁕ ⁕ ⁕

Nic stood in the hallway of the headquarters building of the Defense Language Institute on Presidio of Monterey. Checking her watch, she made sure she was on time. Early was better, and she was in fact almost fifteen minutes early.

0900 hours on the dot.

She'd also made it a point to come in uniform. She wasn't about to be dismissed in civilian clothes. Besides, the uniform and rank had meaning in this world. In the civilian world, not as much. Nic had called Captain Goodwin, leaving a message on his phone about the incident yesterday afternoon. She'd received a return phone call within the hour, and he wasn't happy. The men had already told him their version of the story and made Nic out to be the bad guy. She wasn't worried and frankly didn't care how pissed off Goodwin was. Once he saw the evidence, he would be apologizing to her for his attitude and accusations he'd made over the phone. Twirling the disc around her finger, she smiled. Always be prepared.

The door to Goodwin's office opened and a secretary stepped out. Looking at Nic's name tag, she said, "Miss Caldwell, you're early."

Nic pointed to the birds on her shoulder so the young woman could see them. "Colonel Caldwell."

"Yes, Colonel. This way please."

Entering the office, Nic noticed she wouldn't be meeting Goodwin alone. The two asshats from the shopette jumped up and stood ramrod straight, eyes ahead. They were dressed in their Service C uniforms, looking very tucked away. Clearly a ploy to try to present a different picture than the one they had displayed yesterday.

"At ease, gentlemen." Nic stood in front of the seat across from the desk as the other two took the seats along the wall. The captain still stood and extended his hand. "Colonel Caldwell. I'm Captain Goodwin."

"Captain."

Nic sat down and looked at the captain. She pulled the two men's military IDs and set them on the table in front of her.

"Thanks for coming over, Colonel Caldwell. I'm sure we can clean this up pretty quickly. I understand after talking to you yesterday and then talking to Sinclar and Moffett that there was a misunderstanding yesterday at the…Patel Shopette."

Nic cocked her head and frowned at the captain. "I'm not sure what you've been told, Captain, but this wasn't a misunderstanding. A misunderstanding is when you accidentally pick up a stout beer when your friend said get an ale. A misunderstanding isn't when you put a forty-ouncer in your jacket so you don't have to pay for it."

"I've spoken to my men and they tell me that the reason the counter broke was because you took the bottle from them and slammed it on the counter, demanding they pay for it."

"I see. Lying is punishable by the Uniformed Code of Military Justice. You understand the UCMJ, gentlemen, right?" She gave them a side-eye glance before looking at Goodwin. "Isn't that correct, Captain Goodwin?"

"Yes, ma'am."

"Good. I'm glad we are all in agreement." She pulled the disc out of her hat and placed it on the desk next to the ID cards. "Let me express how disappointed I am, Captain, that you failed to get both sides of the story before making a judgment."

"Ma'am, let me assure you that I am on a fact-finding mission here. These are my men and I have spoken with them extensively about the incident. If you have proof that they are lying, then we can look at that proof. I've sent their platoon leader over to the Patel Shopette to get her side of the story. He should be back in time for the meeting." He looked down at his phone. "I'm not sure what's holding him up, but he should be here soon."

"Well, I have the surveillance video of the incident here. You don't mind if we look at it while we wait for him, do you?"

"Not at all, Colonel."

"Good. Do you have a conference room with a project screen and a DVD player or laptop attached to one?"

"Why a conference room?"

"Well, I don't want there to be any questions about what took place yesterday and on a small screen you might not see everything. I've looked at the surveillance footage and it's quite good. So, do you have a conference room available?"

Goodwin picked up the phone on his desk. "Miss Small, could you see if anyone is in the conference room?"

He set the phone back in its cradle and looked over at the two men. "Gentlemen, you'll wait here while Colonel Caldwell and I look at the footage."

Walking past them, he lowered his head, glared at the men, and whispered, "You better hope this supports your version."

"The conference room is ready, sir."

"Thank you, Miss Small."

He took the lead and walked through a connecting door on the other side of the office. Nic scooped up the ID cards, her hat, and the disc, and followed him into the conference room. She spotted the DVD player and walked over to it.

"Colonel, first I'd like to apologize for my men's behavior. It is completely unacceptable."

"Don't you want to see the video first?"

"Of course."

Nic, stuffed the DVD into the player and hit Play. As she watched events play out on the big conference screen, she was grateful that Benji had started it right at the confrontation. She noticed the speaker in the corner of the screen and turned the sound up. The Patels had sprung for the complete surveillance system. Lucky for Nic, it would only seal the younger men's fate. She watched the events unfold until the real insubordination began.

"Give me your ID cards. You can have them back when I meet with your commanding officer."

"Fuck you. I ain't givin' you shit."

"Oh, Colonel Caldwell. I get the point. The guys screwed up big time."

"Sit down, Captain. You haven't seen the best parts yet."

Captain Goodwin huffed as he sat back down in his seat. He definitely looked defeated.

Nic paused the video. "Nice, huh? I told them I was an officer at the very beginning of this incident. I gave them every opportunity to do the right thing, but they just kept digging." She turned back to the player and hit play again.

Nic was glad Benji had left in his apology for how he tried to protect his parents and their store. It perfectly reflected the difference between the two groups of men. One recognized he had acted inappropriately, and the other two just underscored how their entitlement showed a total lack of respect.

Nic paused the video where the two soldiers were chatting. "Right here, Sinclar is saying something to the effect of, this is what happens when you have sex with a camel." She resumed the video for another few minutes, then stopped again when one of the soldiers on screen was insisting he had no money to pay for the damage.

"You can watch the rest of it when I'm gone. I'd say you have a problem on your hands, Captain. How close was their version of the truth compared to the video?"

Captain Goodwin sat back in his chair, steepled his fingers, and rested them against his lips.

"Look, Captain. I've seen men do strange things in combat. I served in Iraq and most recently in Afghanistan. I've seen men get fired on, wounded, and blown up, and they didn't act like this. So, I'm not about to pretend this didn't happen."

"I understand, Colonel."

Nic sat down across from him. She wasn't about to let him blow her off without finding out what corrective action he planned to take.

"I can put a counseling statement in their file."

"Not good enough."

"Colonel, you're going to ruin their careers

before they even get started."

"Captain, I can't believe you just said that to me, a fellow Marine." Nic scowled at the man. "I've served with some of the finest enlisted personnel one could hope to serve with. I've had to go to men's families and tell them that the Marine Corps was sorry for the loss of their loved one. Are you seriously going to sit here and tell me that these two yahoos represent the best of the Corps?" Nic leaned on the table. "That you trust these two Marines enough to give them a gun and ship them overseas as translators? Because you know that's exactly where their next duty station is going to be, right?"

"I get it, Colonel. I get it."

"Yet you think a counseling statement in their file is enough? They have to be pretty smart to qualify for linguistics. Arabic is a level-three language and one of the harder languages to learn, period. So, they knew exactly what they were doing, Captain."

"Yes, ma'am."

"What do you think their response will be when they get into the field and they have a LGBT officer over them? Clearly, they had no respect for me—they called me a dyke and that I must be in the gay army, right? I caught a big whiff of misogyny rolling off those two men. I would venture to say no woman is safe in the vicinity of those two."

"That's a little harsh, don't you think?" He squirmed and then gave Nic a hard look.

"Is it? Perhaps you can give me a situation where you've had to deal with discriminatory treatment at the hands of your fellow Marines."

"Look, I get where you're going with this, Colonel, I really do—"

"Captain, you keep saying that, but I don't think you really understand where I'm coming from. Perhaps you can bring in your XO and we can have a discussion about how the Marine Corps is taking a hard, wide, systematic look at the treatment of women and LGBT servicemembers and civilians in the Marine Corps. And we haven't even addressed how they treated that shop owner and what they did there."

"Christ, Colonel. You just aren't going to let this go, are you?"

Nic was fuming at his attitude. She was tempted to bring him up on any charge she could think of. Of course she wasn't going to let this go. Women like her deserved better from the Corps, and she wasn't about to let some Captain sweep this under the rug for expediency and to save his own ass. Further, she suspected he would never be this argumentative with a male superior officer.

"Captain, I'd say at this point that this is above your pay grade. Call your XO and a JAG officer. Now."

"Colonel—"

"You had your chance, Captain. Now we'll take care of this through different channels."

"Christ," he said, walking through to his office. She heard him yelling at the two men. "You fucked up big time," came through loud and clear before his door slammed.

Nic didn't trust the captain to follow through on her requests, so she pulled out her cell phone and called the Judge Advocate General's office.

"May I speak to Colonel Tower?…Yes, you can tell her it's Colonel Caldwell…Thank you, I'll wait."

Nic sighed. Why did it always have to come to this? Why couldn't officers just do their jobs? One would think they had plenty of reason to, because their charges' behavior reflected on them as a superior officer. *Superior, my ass.* They had failed the Corps and the United States military, and they weren't going to admit it. Not if they could sweep stuff like this under the rug.

"Hi, Maisy. How are you?…No, I'm not in trouble, but I do have a situation on my hands." Nic explained what had happened yesterday and in the subsequent meeting with Captain Goodwin, highlighting his response to the whole matter.

"Okay. I'll see you in a little while." Nic hung up and then looked at her watch, mumbling, "Great, I'm going to miss lunch with Claire. Shit." She scrolled through her phone and considered just sending a text, but then thought better of it.

"Hi, honey. It looks like you'll have to have lunch without me. I'm still over here at POM and it doesn't look like it's going to be over anytime soon…Yeah. I'll tell you when I get home…Okay, have a good lunch. I'll make it up to you, I promise."

Captain Goodwin walked back into the conference room. "I've called the colonel and he's tied up at the moment, but their platoon sergeant is on his way."

"Good. Just so you know, I've called a JAG officer, Colonel Tower, and she's on her way over, too." Nic walked over to the low cabinet that displayed a coffee maker, water, and a few assorted cookies. Grabbing a water, she motioned it to the captain in question. He shook his head and sat back in his chair. "You could have handled this in another way, Captain, but it seems that you don't like to take charge of your unit. These are serious offenses."

"Yes, ma'am, they are, and I appreciate you bringing them to my attention."

Nic heard a loud voice on the other side of the door ask, "What the hell were you thinking?"

Just as Nic was getting ready to rebuke the captain's patronizing comment, a heavy knock drew their attention to the door. A tall, gangly man in a Service C uniform walked in, took off his cover, and stood at attention. His khaki shirt was ironed to razor-sharp creases, his pressed slacks hung perfectly over his low quarters, and his haircut was high and tight. He was right out of a Marine Corps recruiting poster, Nic thought as she looked at him.

"Staff Sergeant Jerome, this is Colonel Caldwell. She is the one who brought forward some disturbing concerns about Moffett and Sinclar."

He stepped forward and offered his hand. "Ma'am."

"Sergeant Jerome. I'm sorry we have to meet under these circumstances."

"Yes, ma'am."

"Please sit down." Nic offered a seat at the table. Interestingly, he sat a couple of seats away from his commanding officer. "Do you know why Sinclar and Moffett are here, Sergeant?"

He looked at the captain, who nodded at him and then back at Nic. If uncomfortable had a face, it was the spitting image of Sergeant Jerome's. Clearing his throat, he rested his clasped hands on the table and took a deep breath.

"Yes, ma'am."

"How do you know, Sergeant?" The captain had already explained it, but she wanted to hear it for herself.

"I would have been here sooner, sir, but it took longer than I expected down at the shopette. I had to deal with a Benji Patel, who was rather animated about the events yesterday."

"Sergeant Jerome, I heard you saying something to the men in the other office. Mind telling us what you said?" Nic phrased it as a question, but it wasn't one.

Before Jerome could speak, another knock rapped on the door. Miss Small peeked her head around the door.

"Sir, a Colonel Tower is here to see you."

The captain sighed. "Please show Colonel Tower in, Miss Small."

Nic wanted to bust out laughing as the captain said both names in the same sentence. Tower, Small—the irony wasn't lost on Nic as neither woman reflected their surnames. A rather short, petite powerhouse blew through the door.

"Colonel Caldwell, it's good to see you again. Captain…" She looked up at his name tag. "Ah, Captain Goodwin, we haven't had the pleasure of meeting. Sergeant Jerome, I see we have the unfortunate pleasure of meeting again under similar circumstances." She tossed her briefcase on the table and looked over at the coffee maker. "Is there coffee in that thing?"

"Miss Small," the captain bellowed.

"Captain, I'm quite adept at making my own coffee. Thank you." When Miss Small, who was a rather tall woman, walked in, Colonel Tower shooed her off. "I've got this, Miss Small. I'm quite handy with a coffee maker. By the way, he doesn't ask you to make his coffee, does he?"

The captain squirmed a bit as she looked away. "No, ma'am. That isn't in my job description."

"Good, glad to hear it. It's the twenty-first century, for Christ's sake. Men can make their own damn coffee. Women, too." She looked at Nic.

"I don't drink coffee." She smiled at Tower.

"Good for you, it'll stunt your growth." She ran her hand down her uniform like one of those women on a game show showing off the prizes, then laughed at her own joke. This was why Nic liked Maisy so much. She didn't take crap from anyone below a one-star general.

"Now tell me what the hell is going on here."

"Maybe it would be better if you saw it with your own eyes, Colonel," Nic said, hitting the remote and starting the video.

Nic watched as everyone reacted in their own way to the surveillance tape. Sergeant Jerome's face flushed in anger. The captain looked like he wished he was anywhere else as he fiddled with his watchband when he wasn't watching the video. Colonel Tower was expressionless. She took notes almost as if she was blindfolded—quick scribbles without even looking.

Nic was impressed.

"Well, that's a shit show. Are those the two men waiting in your office, Captain?"

"Yes, ma'am."

"Well…" She looked down at her notes and scribbled some more. "Considering the threat against Colonel Caldwell, the derogatory comments made to her, the destruction of private property—good thing they didn't walk out with that forty in their jacket—the outright disgusting way they acted…I'd be interested in what you think is appropriate punishment considering you're their commanding officer, Captain Goodwin."

He shrugged. "I've offered my opinion to Colonel

Caldwell and that didn't seem to sit well with her, so I'm at a loss. I'd hate to see a stupid incident like this ruin two careers."

"I see." She looked at Sergeant Jerome. "Sergeant? What are your thoughts on the matter?"

"Ma'am?"

"You're their platoon leader. I'm sure you have an opinion on these two gentlemen."

"Yes, ma'am."

"I want to remind you, Sergeant, that you and I have a history with these two individuals. They are not strangers to me."

"Yes, ma'am. I don't believe this is a case for reduction in rank, confined to barracks, or a counseling statement in their file."

Nic looked over at Captain Goodwin, who didn't look at anyone. He just stared straight ahead, emotionless.

"I see, Sergeant. And why is that?"

"Moffett was a Lance Corporal already and was busted down to Private First Class, and that didn't seem to teach him a lesson."

"And Sinclair?"

Sergeant Jerome shook his head. "His file is clean. Nothing. I just think Moffett is a bad influence on the young man."

"That's unfortunate, Sergeant." Colonel Tower nodded to Jerome briskly and turned to Nic.

"First, Colonel Caldwell, let me apologize for their behavior and what they said to you. Clearly, they didn't learn anything during basic training. They do not reflect Marine Corps values and what the Marine Corps stands for. As for their behavior in the public sector, this is a black mark for anyone who represents the military. If this was the Patels' only exposure to servicemembers, then their impression of the military would be seriously tainted. As for what I think should be done, there are regulations that need to be followed. This isn't an incident where a counseling statement would apply." Picking up the disc, she said, "I'm taking this as evidence. I am recommending they be remanded to barracks and not allowed to leave for the time being."

Everyone stood as Colonel Tower stood. "This is unacceptable behavior. What should be their punishment will be determined by a JAG court. My recommendation would be at a minimum an Article Fifteen, perhaps a dishonorable discharge on a failure to adapt, but that won't be my decision to make. Captain, I'll leave it to you to explain to the men what's going on. I'll also leave it to you to draft the paperwork on the remand to barracks. As for the rest, I'll be in touch. I'll see about getting them some representation."

"I appreciate you coming down on such short notice, Colonel," Nic said.

"I'm glad you called. Has anyone talked to the Patels?"

Sergeant Jerome raised his hand. "I did earlier. Mrs. Patel didn't want to press charges. She said Colonel Caldwell handled it and she appreciates her help in the matter. The son, Benji, he's a different story."

"Is he old enough, or does he have part ownership in the business?" Colonel Tower looked at Nic and then at Sergeant Jerome. Both shrugged. "Okay, well we'll deal with that if it comes up." Shouldering her briefcase, she extended her hand to Nic. "Again, Colonel Caldwell, I'm sorry that you had to be a part of all of this."

"Thank you, Colonel Tower. I don't believe these young men are indicative of the fine men and women we are putting out as Marines."

"I agree. Captain, I'll need your report on my desk by tomorrow. I assume you can handle that?"

"Yes, ma'am."

"Good. Now if someone can tell me the way to the ladies' room, I've got another appointment to get to."

"I can show you, Colonel Tower. I've got an appointment that I'm already late for. Captain, Sergeant, thank you for your time." Nic handed the ID cards to Sergeant Jerome. "I'm not sure how you want to handle these, but I leave them in your capable hands."

"Thank you, Colonel. Ma'am, I'd like to apologize on behalf of my men. I'm sorry for the things they said to you yesterday."

"Thank you, Sergeant. But you aren't responsible for their behavior and I would feel better if the apology was coming from them."

"Yes, ma'am."

Nic walked past the young men who seemed to take it all in stride if playing video games on their phones was any indication.

Clueless, utterly clueless, Nic thought as she stopped to look at each of them.

"What?" Moffett said, looking up from his phone at Nic.

"Moffett," Sergeant Jerome barked.

Nic waved him off. "It's fine, Sergeant. If I had any thought of changing my mind, he's sealed his own fate."

"I'm sorry, Colonel."

"I know. Me, too." Nic followed Colonel Tower

out into the hallway. She cocked her head to the left. "Bathroom's this way."

"What a motley crew," Maisy said. "What is up with that captain? He acted like he couldn't care less about what happened."

"You got that sense, too?" Nic shook her head. "I suspect he knows more about these two young men than he was letting on. Maybe he's covering for them, I'm not sure, but Sergeant Jerome seemed to be done with them."

"Without giving too much away. I can tell you he has definitely had his fill of those two."

"That bad, huh?"

"Oh yeah. Lunch?"

"I thought you said you had an appointment?"

"I say that when I need to get out of a meeting, and I wasn't going to be waiting around to see if that captain grew a spine."

"I'll remember that next time I have a meeting with the commandant." Nic smiled. She could learn a lot from Maisy.

Chapter Eight

*C*laire?" Nic tossed her hat and briefcase on a chair and started untucking her shirt. "Claire?"

Nothing.

Her first month of teaching had gone as well as could be expected. Most of her students were seasoned officers from all branches of the service and other countries, with a few of what she would term "newbies." Her classes were on the counterterrorism track with insight into how to work with ethnic factions in country.

Today though, she'd been invited to give a talk to the Junior Reserve Officers' Training Corps at a local high school. Claire's student teaching gig was at a high school down the valley, and Nic had been offered up so the students could interact with a female Marine officer. Claire thought it would be good for the girls in the class to see a woman in uniform, and Rod, as the JROTC coordinator, agreed.

Staff Sergeant Montanez was a retired Green Beret. This had been her first and only interaction with Montanez as she surveyed him and his office. He was squared away with his dress uniform and beret, and his office was impressive with a set of crossed 9mm Berettas with pearl handles. A gift from a grateful unit. ArComs—Army Commendations—and unit citations lined the wall and didn't have a speck of dust on them.

He explained that he'd grown up in the Salinas Valley and running the JROTC program was his way of giving back to a community he felt needed the structure and discipline the military had given a lost kid like him.

She liked talking to young people about military service. It had been a stepping-stone out of a small town and small-minded family that would have made her life miserable until she acquiesced and married someone they approved of.

It had been an eye-opener when she walked into class. Young men and a few women, barely older than children, dressed in Army-green uniforms sat in neat rows. They all stood, ramrod straight, at the same time, and saluted the minute she walked into the room. She looked at them all, uniforms with razor creases and shined low quarters. They didn't even look old enough to drive, let alone think about enlisting.

"At ease. Please, sit down."

As a group, the students relaxed and sat down. She introduced herself and told the students a little about what she did for a living. She played the college ROTC card heavily. It was her own experiences as an ROTC cadet that had given her the ability to go to college. Finally, after talking about flight school and giving them the quick version of deployment, it was time for Q and A.

"So, who has questions?"

Every hand in the room shot up. She pointed to a young man who looked rather reserved. She liked to pick those students because she could see her younger self in them.

"Colonel Caldwell, have you ever seen a terrorist?"

"Well, I'm not sure. I've seen men who I thought

were friendly to the United States do some bad things at a base I was at in Afghanistan. It cost several servicemen their lives. So, I guess the answer would be yes."

"Did you kill him?" A young man followed.

"No."

"Why not? Man, when I get over there, I'm gonna kill me a bunch of terrorists," he replied, punching his hand then high-fiving a few boys around him.

Nic looked at the instructor, who shrugged and smiled at her. Ah, that's how this was going to go. Well, the Army needed strong backs and weak minds, she told herself.

"How about we take another question?" Nic pointed to a girl who had kept her hand up the whole time.

"Was flight school hard?"

"Do you want to fly helicopters?" She asked the young girl.

"Maybe. What kind of grades do you have to get to go to flight school?"

"Well, I enrolled in ROTC in college, and from there I went to my basic course and then flight school. I always wanted to fly, so this was the only way I could afford to make my dreams come true. I won't lie, it was hard, and you have to work hard and do well in college, but it was worth it."

"Do you have any tattoos?" a kid yelled out. "Staff Sergeant Montanez has tattoos."

"Okay, let's ask Colonel Caldwell questions about the military," Montanez said.

"I don't have any tattoos, but I do have some cool Marine Corps swag if anyone is interested. Any other questions?"

Another dozen hands went up. Nic smiled. Their excitement was contagious, and she loved talking about how the Corps had changed her life. Letting a young man or woman know what they could achieve if they just set their minds to it was exhilarating. After half an hour, Nic got the high sign from Montanez. Time was over.

"Again, I have some Marine Corps swag if anyone is interested." She motioned to the desk where she'd laid out pens, hats, T-shirts, and some recruiting brochures. Everything was snapped up before the staff sergeant had made his way to her.

"Hey, thanks a lot, Colonel. Sorry about the tattoo question."

She brushed it off. "Don't worry about it. You can never anticipate some questions."

"Yeah, well I really appreciate you coming all the way down here and talking to them. I really like to have them talk to someone, and when Rod said you'd make a great speaker, he wasn't kidding. I bet you've got some stories we could swap over a beer sometime."

"Well, they aren't stories for young people like this, that's for sure. Do you talk to them about your time in the first Gulf War?"

"Oh, sure. They eat that stuff up."

"Ah." She shouldered her bag and stuck her hand out. "Hey, thanks for inviting me to speak to the students. They had great questions. If you want to take a tour of the Naval Postgraduate School, I'm sure I can arrange something for you."

"Really? That would be great."

"Sure." Nic reached into her bag and pulled out her wallet. "Here's my card. Just give me some notice and I'll see what I can do."

"Nice, thanks. The kids would really like it. I know I would." He turned to the students. "Attention." He barked out the command.

Students stood straight up and turned toward Nic.

"How do we show our appreciation to Colonel Caldwell for her time?"

All the students snapped a salute and held it until she returned it.

"Have a great weekend," she said, lowering her hand.

"Yes, ma'am."

"At ease," Montanez said as she walked out of the room.

Chapter Nine

*O*fficer assistance needed, possible ten-fifty-six Adam at 1356 General Joseph Way."

"Ten-four. Unit twelve in route."

"Great, another header off the balcony. Probably had too much to drink and then got depressed because his girlfriend said something he didn't like and…" Murdoch made a diving motion with his hand. "Boosshh."

"That's so sensitive of you, sir."

"What? You better get used to it. We are talking walking hormones. Add alcohol and one little comment, and the snowflakes melt."

Cece shook her head as she wrote the information down.

County communications came back on the radio. "Roger, RP is girlfriend Melody Griggs. You'll find her at the residence. Rescue is on the way."

"Ten-four."

Cece hit the lights and sirens. At this time of night there probably wouldn't be a lot of traffic, but once they got to the address kids would be piling out of their houses to see the commotion.

Murdoch killed the sirens. "No need to go full Hollywood, Ramirez. Besides, it will just draw the flies to the yard."

Cece shook her head. Murdoch was a portrait in tact. Hopefully, he didn't lead the sensitivity training for the unit. She could see it now.

"Hey how's everyone feel about the LGBTQ students on campus?"

Everyone would give a thumbs-up.

"Good. How about students of color?"

Thumbs-up.

"Good. Let's get out there and play nice in the schoolyard. Have a nice day."

Hopefully the chief could see Murdoch had his limitations. Besides, it was state-mandated training. Even the Army required it on a yearly basis.

"Hey." Murdoch snapped his fingers in front of Cece's face. "Earth to Ramirez. Make sure you have that fluorescent vest on when you get out of the car. I want you to be seen and respected."

Yeah, like a fluorescent stripe exudes respect.

"I'll let you check the vic and I'll talk to the girlfriend and get her statement."

Pussy. She watched him weave the cruiser through the few students who had started to congregate on the street. He popped the siren after one student didn't bother to get out of his way. The bird was his reward from the student. That gesture seemed to follow Murdoch everywhere.

"Asshat," the kid yelled at Murdoch.

"Yeah, that's our future right there," Murdoch said, watching him in the rearview mirror. "Stick around, kid. I got you on my dance card later."

"You probably scared him with the horn, LT," Cece said, trying to defend the kid's action.

"Everyone else can get out of the way but that asshat. Seriously, Ramirez. These kids don't need you to protect them. Trust me, their mommies and daddies have lawyers and have no problem using them. You wait, your time's coming when one of these little shits screams police brutality when you go to arrest them."

While she hated to admit it, he was probably right. No matter how well intended she would be, it was the same as it was in the Army: no good deed went unpunished.

"There. That's the address." He pointed to a woman who was standing beside a van, crying and gesturing to an officer.

Rescue had just arrived on scene, unloaded a gurney with all their gear on it, and ran past Cece. Another unit had pulled up and was putting up crime scene tape to keep the lookie-loos away from the house and van. Cece steeled herself. She'd seen dead bodies before, but not an attempted suicide. Dispatch hadn't said whether it was a gunshot wound, hanging, or overdose. Cece tried to prepare for the worst, but realized she wasn't sure which that was.

Pulling the crime scene tape over her head, she pushed a student who'd ducked under it backward past the tape.

"Out. Go home. This doesn't concern you," she said as the guy tried to look around her. "I said, go home or I'm arresting you for interfering in a crime scene."

"What happened?"

"None of your business. Who's your Resident Advisor?" Cece keyed the mic. "Dispatch, can you call Res Life and get the RA on call out here?"

"Roger."

"Move, now." She snapped on a pair of latex gloves and stared the kid down until he finally turned around and walked away.

Stepping to the side of the van, Cece asked.

"How's the victim?"

"He's alive." The EMT handed a pill bottle to Cece. "Sleeping pill overdose."

Cece looked at the label. *Rod White.* Didn't ring a bell. "Is there a note, or…"

"Inside the van. On the dash." He tossed his head in the direction of the van.

Cece was shocked at the extent of the damage to Rod White's body. His right hand and leg were missing, and his left hand was barely mobile. How he was able to drive, let alone try to commit suicide, was a mystery. Where the mind wants to go, the body finds a way. She was told that once when she had seen a soldier who'd had his legs practically blown off drag himself a dozen yards to save himself. Nothing surprised her anymore when it came to the determination of people.

Cece jumped out of the way of the gurney running toward the ambulance. She heard the EMT say, "It's all yours, Officer."

"Thanks." She pulled her flashlight out and looked around inside the van. She marveled at the magnificent piece of engineering she found inside. His wheelchair was locked in place. The gas and brakes were hand operated, and the interior of the cabin was spotless with the exception of a cell phone, a note, and flowers. There was a card on the flowers and the envelope was made out to Melody. Stepping on the running board, she looked up on the dash and picked up the note by a corner.

Cece frowned. She recognized a name in the note. What were the odds?

Chapter Ten

Nic looked at Cece standing in her doorframe, her body backlit from the porch light. It had been a while since she'd seen Cece, so it was a surprise seeing her in uniform. The words were like an echo in Nic's mind: "Rod White tried to commit suicide tonight."

"Come in, Cece." Nic waved her through to the living room. Claire threaded her hand through Nic's arm and grabbed her biceps. She recognized a squeeze of reassurance thrown in for good measure.

"How?" Nic tried to offer Cece a seat on the sofa but she begged off, preferring to stand. She recognized the dispassionate look on her face immediately; she'd seen it far too often in Afghanistan. She'd thought Cece might be at her house to talk about Benji and the incident at the market. "I can't believe it. I just talked to him about his upcoming wedding. He wanted me to help, be part of his..." Nic paused. Rod's fiancée. Nic crossed her fingers in hopes he hadn't taken her life and the baby's, too. "His fiancée, is she—"

"She's fine. Unfortunately, she's the one who found Mr. White locked in his van." Cece pulled a pen and pad from her chest pocket and flipped the pad open. "How do you know Mr. White, Nic?"

"Group."

"Group?"

"Yeah, sorry. We were in the same veteran's

support group. He leads it. I met him when I attended a few sessions."

"I see. So that's what happened to him?" She motioned to her own arm and face.

"You mean the injuries?"

She nodded, all business, as she scribbled on her pad. "Yep. It looked pretty bad."

"Yeah, well you know that's what happens when a soldier is hit with a bomb."

"Shame, so young."

"Yeah. He's just a kid."

She was having a hard time wrapping her mind around the fact that the young man she'd just talked to last night had tried to take his own life. Sure he was struggling, but they all were in their own way. Rod, though, presented a well-put-together package for someone so young dealing with life-altering injuries. Nic hadn't pegged him as a suicide risk.

Christ. Group.

Suicide had a habit of breeding more suicide. While Nic had left group, she was sure this would rock their recovery.

"How did it happen?" Nic asked.

"Pills. We found a bottle of painkillers in the van."

"At home?"

Cece shook his head. "In his vehicle. Left a note. Said he didn't want her to have to clean it up. Left a note for you, too, Colonel. That's why I'm here." She held up a clear plastic evidence bag with a handwritten note in it. "Did he say anything to you?"

Nic shook her head. A note for her? Nic held out her hand. "Can I see the note?"

"Sure. It's evidence. So, I can't allow you to take

it out of the bag."

"I see." Nic felt her knees start to buckle, so she sat down. "I just talked to him last night on the phone."

"How did he seem?"

"Fine."

"Fine?"

"Yeah, he sounded good. He's getting married, and we talked about Melody and the baby. She was so excited about the baby. He was a little apprehensive, but thrilled."

"Did he say anything else?"

Nic ran her hands through her hair and then scrubbed her face. This couldn't be happening. He had been fine when they talked. She kept telling herself that over and over again.

And still, suicide attempt.

Nic shook her head again, racking her brain for anything from last night's conversation.

"He said he was having some pain, but nothing a painkiller wouldn't handle, he said."

"We found an empty bottle of painkillers on the dash of the van. Seems he might have been taking more than he should have along with the sleeping pills, and he was definitely trying to check out. Know anything about that? How did he seem on the phone?"

"Yeah, no. I mean, I didn't know he was abusing painkillers, if that's what you're asking. I told you he was fine. Upbeat, happy."

Cece handed Nic the note.

"Can I get you some coffee, Cece?"

"Sure, that would be great, Claire. Long night ahead. I have to go back and interview the fiancée."

Christ. Nic wanted to be there for Melody and the baby when Cece went back over. From what Rod had told her, it would take a day for Melody's family to come in and she wanted to make sure Rod had all the help he needed. She'd call the VA and see about getting a counselor out to see Rod.

"Here you go. I put it in a travel cup so you can take it with you." Claire offered a smile as she handed the cup to Cece.

"Thanks. I appreciate it."

"No problem."

Nic looked at the note. It was simple.

Nic,

I'm so sorry. I know I've let you down. Please watch out for Melody and tell her this isn't her fault. I love her and my son, I just think this would be easier on them if I wasn't around.

Sorry buddy.

Rod

Nic tapped the note against her leg. The rate of suicide in those returning from Afghanistan was high. PTSD, injuries, and coming home less that the person who left were all part of a brew that made the servicemember ripe for suicide if they didn't get counseling and come to terms with their new reality. Nic knew that all too well as she dealt with her own demons. She'd be lying if she didn't admit to herself that she had considered whether Claire and Grace would be better off without her and her baggage, but it was when she was at her lowest that those thoughts anchored themselves in her soul. She had to work every day to keep them tucked away in the box she had for them. They only came out when she was in counseling and felt like she could control them.

Diligence, hard work, and counseling for both her and Claire had kept her on this side of sane. But if she was being honest, she could easily step over that line. She was always just a foothold away from slipping.

"Okay." Cece pulled a business card from her breast pocket. "If you think of anything, can you give me a call at my work number?"

"Sure. Um, do you know where they've taken him?" Nic knew the protocol for a military attempted suicide, but civilians probably did things differently.

"He's been admitted to Community Hospital over in Monterey. He's probably on a fifty-one-fifty hold. Once they run a tox screen and determine if he was under the influence, they'll most likely let his fiancée see him after a shrink sees him first."

"What about the van?"

"We had it towed. It had some stuff inside that we need to look at. Once we've gone through it, we'll release it to the fiancée."

"Melody."

"Excuse me?"

"His fiancée's name is Melody Griggs."

It was the first time Nic saw Cece get a little shaken as she corrected her. "Once we're done going over it, we'll release it to Ms. Griggs."

"Ramirez, we need to get a move on." A tall cop poked his head around the door.

"Okay." She turned back to Nic. "Sorry, I have to go."

"Thanks, Cece."

"Let me know if you think of anything," she

said as she left. She stopped at the stoop. "I'm really sorry, Nic. I know this is hard, but at least he wasn't successful."

Nic choked up. She was thrown by the suicide attempt. "Thank you, Officer Ramirez." Nic said with the other officer still standing in her doorway.

"Yes, ma'am."

Closing the door, she leaned against it suddenly feeling the weight of Rod on her shoulders. Now she knew what it felt like being on the other side of an inform. God, she hoped she sounded a little more compassionate when she told families the bad news and listened to their varied, unpredictable, and emotional reactions.

"Honey?"

Nic was trying to piece together her conversation with Rod. Had he said something she missed? Did he ask for help, and was she so into her own pain that she'd overlooked a cry for help?

"Honey?" Claire rested her chin on Nic's shoulder and wrapped her arms around Nic's body. "Sweetheart?"

"Huh?"

"Honey, this isn't your fault."

Nic looked at Claire, her eyes welling up with tears. "I just talked to him last night, Claire. He didn't say anything. Nothing. How could he do this to Melody and the baby?"

Claire shrugged. "I wish I knew, hon."

"He was so happy about the baby. They'd found out it was a boy." Nic buried her face in her hands and started to sob. A boy. They were going to have a boy. He said they were going to name it after him, against his protests of course, but Melody insisted. Family tradition and all, Rod had told her.

"Honey, I think we should go over and check on Melody." Claire rubbed Nic's back and rested her cheek on her head. "Maybe I can help."

Nic nodded. Claire not only knew what Melody was going through, she knew what was to come. Nic thought she herself had a good idea of what Rod was going through, and yet she couldn't reason with suicide. It was a permanent solution to a temporary problem.

"I'll get Grace and take her over to Mrs. Stoddard's house. I'm sure she won't mind watching her."

"Thanks," Nic said, not really listening. She struggled to get up under the weight of the news. Her back bowed, but she managed to shrug on her jacket and grab the keys to her car. What would she say to Melody? The agony of attempted suicide was heavy. It was something that defied reason, especially to those left behind wondering what they had done to make someone take such actions. Nic replayed their conversation over and over again, but nothing stood out.

Nothing.

Maybe Melody would have some answers. Then again, she didn't need the third degree right now. Nic was sure the police had done that trying to get answers.

Isabella

Chapter Eleven

The trip to Rod's house had been a silent procession. As Nic rounded the corner, she spotted a news truck on the street and the neighbors all hanging out in their front yards. Rod lived in family housing at CSUMB. He and Melody were both getting their degrees, and the school offered family housing to those students. Pulling in behind a car in the drive, Nic killed the engine and sat, staring at the reporter on the stoop who was knocking on the door.

"Fucking vultures," Nic whispered.

"I recognize that woman. She's from that independent conservative station. And that one…" Claire pointed to a man standing down below, staring at his phone. "That's Hank Spelling, reporter for the *Monterey Tribune*." Nic followed Claire's gaze.

Someone walking up the drive caught Nic's attention. "Oh, great. It's Mr. Overshare from group." She wondered how he'd found out so quickly. It didn't matter; whatever he said would be fodder for the news media. If it bleeds it leads, wasn't that the saying? Nic noticed he had walked right up to Spelling, avoiding the female reporter entirely, and started talking. A diversion. Well, at least he was good for something.

"Come on, let's go around back and go in that way," Nic said, pulling Claire's hand and easing her out of the car.

Quietly, Nic gently pushed the door shut and

slipped under the ivy trestle. The pea gravel crunched under her steps, but it only made her quicken her pace, pulling Claire along. She didn't want to be caught, and she sure as hell didn't want to answer anyone's questions about Rod.

She peered through the sheer curtain at the slider and saw Melody sobbing on the couch as she stared at her cell phone. The room was almost dark, but the light of her phone was just enough to see her face. Tapping on the door, Nic waved at Melody, but Melody didn't move.

"Melody, it's Nic."

Melody ran to the door, swung it wide, and leapt into Nic's embrace.

Nic froze for a moment before she scooped Melody up and took her inside.

"I'm so sorry, Melody. The cops just left. I came as soon as I heard." Nic rambled, not knowing exactly what to say. Claire touched Nic's back. "Oh, this is my wife, Claire."

"Hi, Melody. I'm so sorry we had to meet under these circumstances." Claire offered a smile and then sat on the other side of Melody. "I'm Claire."

"Hi, Claire. I'm Melody Griggs, Rod's girlfriend." Melody waved them over to the couch.

"I don't know what happened, Colonel. I mean, everything seemed fine earlier. He said he'd talked to you and you'd agreed to be his best mate…" Nic smiled at the reference. Melody had served with a British unit for a short time over in Afghanistan and had picked up a few phrases that clearly had stuck with her.

"I was honored that he asked me." Nic patted Melody's hand.

"He loves you, Nic. Said you understand him."

"He's a great kid." Nic chuckled at the reference Rod tolerated. Rank had its privilege, she'd told him one night after group.

"What happened, Melody?"

Melody shrugged. She looked up at the ceiling trying to compose herself. "All I can think of is that he had a conversation with his dad earlier today. He seemed pissed when he got off the phone. I asked him what was wrong, and he just said that he hated his dad." Melody wiped her eyes. "He said he needed some air and space, so I didn't say anything when he went outside. I figured he'd come in when he calmed down."

Melody lovingly rubbed her bulging stomach and sobbed harder.

"It's okay, Melody. Have you called your family? Can I do anything?" Nic looked over at Claire and offered a weak smile. Her empathy was lacking ever since she'd left her duties in San Diego, so she looked to Claire for comfort skills. She didn't have a clue as to what Melody was going through, but she definitely knew how Rod was feeling right now.

"Yeah, I called my mom and she's on her way. My dad has to work, so he can't come. He said if I really needed him to be here, he'd come down."

"Okay. I want to see Rod. Are you up to it?"

"I'm not sure they will let us." Melody wiped her swollen eyes.

"Well, I'd like to try, if that's okay." Nic had a need to see her friend and try to help.

Melody nodded but didn't commit to anything. She sat, her hands folded over the slight bulge of her belly, staring down at it.

"Melody, if you just want me to stay here and Nic can go check on Rod, I can do that if you want." Claire moved to the other side of Melody and rested her hand over hers, then put Melody's head on her shoulder. "I know it's tough, but you still have Rod."

"Yeah, but which Rod? The one who wants to kill himself? Or the Rod who was excited to find out he was having a son?"

"I wish I had the answers, honey. The good news is, he didn't succeed. He needs help and we can get that for him. Right, Nic?"

Claire stroked Melody's hair and offered a weak smile to Nic. This was Claire in a nutshell.

A sheepdog. A protector at heart. Something beyond just being a parent, but someone who looked out for others.

"We'll get him help, Melody. I promise. I can make a few calls and we can get someone to come and see him. But first we have to find out if he's even open to that right now."

Melody nodded, eyes closed. Long eyelashes held tight to the tears that wanted to fall but resisted.

Nic needed to get to Community Hospital as soon as possible. It wasn't exactly a bastion of services for veterans, so she wanted to be there for Rod if he needed an immediate advocate. Maybe a friendly face could help the troubled man. Nic shook her head. *Man.* He had always looked like a boy to her, and she guessed he always would. However, now he'd taken a man-size decision to try to end his life.

In group, they'd always talked about reaching out if someone was suicidal.

Ask for help.

It isn't a sign of weakness.

Tell someone you're struggling.

We've all been there.

We want to help.

All were phrases he'd said over and over again to those who struggled with their PTSD, acceptance, and life in general. It was hard moving from a sheepdog role to being a sheep, from the head of the house to someone who needed help with everyday tasks. War was an ugly business, and this side of it was well hidden behind that magic curtain no one liked to talk about.

She knew all too well the struggle of reentry. She and Claire'd had several power struggles as they tried to navigate their way back to a normal relationship. It felt as if Claire had grown and become stronger and Nic…Well, when you can barely tie your shoes some mornings it doesn't make for a great case of taking back your role as provider, protector, and wife.

"I'll walk you out, honey," Claire said. "Melody, I'll be right back."

Melody only nodded, her hands still cradling her stomach. They headed to the front door, seeing that the press and lookie-loos had all gotten impatient or bored and had abandoned their posts on the lawn.

The day's sky had turned a beautiful shade of orange as the sunset started its dazzling display. Nic would never tire of watching it dip into the ocean. She and Claire had spent many an evening sitting just at the edge of the world watching Mother Nature make them all envious of her talents.

Nic laced her fingers between Claire's and pulled her into a tight embrace as she leaned against the SUV. The warmth of Claire's body was like a soothing balm to Nic's soul. Hugging her tighter, she felt Claire's breath on her neck as Nic lowered her head closer for a kiss that sent a chill through Nic.

Nic had only just recently been able to lay bare

her soul and be more open with Claire. She still had her moments, but she was trying hard to keep those terrors tucked away in a box until she was ready to deal with them.

"I'll stay with her until you get back." Claire's warm cheek rubbed against Nic's.

"What about Grace?"

"I'll call Millie and let her know I'll be a little longer. Besides, she wanted me to give her an update."

"Millie?"

"General Stoddard's wife. I told you about her. I met her at the commissary and then ran into her at the Women's March. Remember?"

"Right, right. I wasn't fully listening when you were laying out the details of where you were taking Grace." Nic panicked. "You didn't tell her about Rod, did you?"

Claire rested her hand on Nic's chest and smiled up at her. "I only told her that there was an emergency with someone you go to group with. I didn't give her all of the gory details, honey."

"Thanks. I know Rod's not in anymore, but there is still a piece of me that wants to keep this stuff out of the military's hands. Besides, it's private and not my story to tell."

"Sweetheart…"

"I know, I know."

"This hit too close to home." Claire rested her head against Nic's chest.

The heat of their bodies buffeted the night chill that was setting in. The fog had done its job, leaving a layer of glistening wet all over everything. Nic rested her head on Claire's and wondered for the umpteenth time how she'd been so lucky to catch such a wonderful woman.

"The sooner I go, the sooner I'll get back, sweetheart."

Claire snuggled one last time before she pulled out of Nic's grasp. "I'll be waiting."

Nic's lips lingered on Claire's, wishing they were home and hiding under the covers that kept the world at bay. At home they could close everything out and pretend that only she, Grace, and Claire mattered. Unfortunately, that was a fantasy not to be realized anytime soon.

"I'll call if I get delayed."

"Okay. I love you."

Nic offered a slight smile.

"This isn't you, Nic. You're not Rod, sweetheart."

"I know. But what's the difference between us? He also has so much to live for, Claire, I just don't understand."

"Just be there to listen, honey. No judgment."

Nic let her fingers slide through Claire's grasp. "No judgment."

Nic pulled her jacket tighter around herself, replacing the warmth Claire had taken with her. She waited until Claire was inside and safely tucked in before she left.

The twenty minutes to the hospital turned out to be a dress rehearsal of what she would say to Rod. Her heart ached for the young man. He had so much life ahead of him, and yet he'd only looked for a way out instead. Depression, desperation, and defeat; the three Ds had a way of worming their way into your brain. While the logical side told someone to ignore that voice in their head, the emotional side was alive and well and doing a fast-track dance to override the other voice. She played her last conversation with Rod over and over in her head.

"Colonel."

"Rod. How are you?"

"I'm good. I just thought I'd pass on the good news."

Silence.

A sniffle on the other end of the phone.

"Rod, you okay?"

"It's a boy, Colonel. Melody's having a boy."

"That's great, but she's only what…four months pregnant? Can they see that plumbing already?"

Nic knew little about pregnancy and wanted to keep it that way. She never had any urges to be pregnant or have a baby herself, but she and Claire had talked about it recently. Claire felt a baby would be more cement to their relationship. That, she didn't understand.

"We had an amnio done. I wanted to make sure the baby would be all right. You know with my injuries and all the meds I'm on, I didn't want to put Melody or the baby at risk."

"Amnio?"

"Amniocentesis. It's a process where they stick a needle into the amniotic fluid and test it for different stuff."

"Ah, gotcha. So, you're having a son. That's great news, Rod. Congrats."

"Thanks, Colonel. I can't believe I'm going to have a little Rod running around in a few months. It's…well, it's a miracle. I honestly can't believe it. I'm gonna call my dad with the good news later. I hope he's as proud as I am, I mean…well, you know. A son and all."

"I'm sure he's going to be thrilled. You'll be carrying on your and his name."

"Yeah, well since he's going to be the first grandson, I'm pretty sure he's gonna be excited. I can't wait to tell him."

Nic wasn't as sure as Rod was when it came to his dad being excited. His father had consistently voiced his disappointment in Rod, at least that's what Rod had told her. He had told Rod on one particular occasion that he thought Rod would have been better off dead. Funny how a career military man could turn on his son who had almost given his life for his country. Then again, Rod's dad probably would have felt better with a big military funeral and burial at Arlington. That would give him his only chance at bragging rights, considering the man had never seen combat in his twenty years in the Army.

Asshole.

Nic mindlessly turned into the hospital parking lot and found a spot. The fog curled around the trees, lampposts, and the lone security shack that lacked someone posted inside. As she exited the vehicle, Nic grabbed her jacket tighter, pulling her collar up on her neck. She hoped it would shield her from the onslaught of feelings that was about to come.

Nic weaved her way to the nurse's station in a practically vacant emergency department, where they gave her the runaround until she told a white lie and informed then that she was Rod White's emergency contact. Someone finally offered up the information that Rod had regained consciousness and was now resting in the Garden Pavilion, CHOMP's inpatient mental health department. Nic had seen a counselor at this hospital when she returned to Monterey, so she was pretty familiar with the Pavilion, but not the secure portion. Making her way through the maze of hallways, she landed at the security doors of the restricted ward. Pushing the buzzer, Nic was greeted by a voice from over the intercom. "Good evening. How can I help you?"

Nic could see the nurse staring at her monitor.

"I received an emergency call that a friend has been admitted. I went to emergency and they told me he was here. I'd like to see him if that's possible."

"And your friend's name is…"

"White. Rod White."

"One moment, please."

The door buzzed and she was let through. Nic could see the dark floor of the mental ward past the bright lights that surrounded the nurses' station.

"I'd like to see Rod White, please."

"Hmm, let me see if we have him. Ah, here he is. Attempted suicide."

Nic didn't flinch at the hint of disdain that laced the nurse's voice. The woman had probably seen it all, but Nic couldn't help but wonder at the quick judgment apparent in her tone.

"He is in a room for the night and—"

"I'd like to see him, please."

"I'm not sure I can allow that."

"Why don't you go and ask him? I'm sure he'll see me."

"And you are?"

"Colonel Nic Caldwell." Nic pulled her ID to prove she was who she said she was.

"His commanding officer?"

"I'd like to see him, please. I'm sure you can make that happen. I'm here on behalf of his pregnant fiancée and his family who can't be here." The fact that she wasn't his commanding officer was a minor detail, and she wasn't actually lying as she didn't answer the direct question. She wasn't leaving until she saw Rod, so she wouldn't take no for an answer.

"I'll see what I can do. Can you have a seat over there, please?"

Nic stood at the station instead. A few minutes passed when a scholarly-looking young man in a button-down shirt, tie, sweater, and jeans came out. He scratched his beard as he looked at Nic. Coming around the counter, he extended his hand toward Nic.

"Hi, Colonel Caldwell, I'm Dr. Tishman. I understand you're here to see Rod White."

"I am."

"Great, well can you follow me? I'd like to discuss his condition with you before you see him."

Nic noticed a few patients roaming the hallways as she and the doctor made their way through the dark corridors. They weren't dressed in hospital gowns, but in sweats and slippers as they slowly walked. Mindless wasn't exactly the correct word, but they seemed to be wandering with no purpose. Nic heard a TV down the hall, and glanced into a room with chairs in a circle occupied by a few occupants. Nic recognized a group meeting when she saw one.

"In here, please."

A well-lit office with little in the way of furnishings greeted her. Dr. Tishman sat behind the generic desk and opened a folder.

"We admitted Mr. White tonight on a fifty-one-fifty." The doctor looked down at Rod's file and continued. "I don't have to tell you that he tried to overdose on painkillers today. The officers felt they had no choice but to fifty-one-fifty him, especially with his physical condition. I've done an assessment, and while he is responding favorably, I'd like to keep him here for at least another forty-eight hours."

Nic knew the code for involuntary commitment to a mental health facility. Nic's only other experience with a suicidal incident had happened in Afghanistan, the tour that kept on giving. She'd had to deal with a green-on-blue attack when a trusted Afghan soldier attacked a US military member when she was stationed in Afghanistan, and it had left an indelible mark on her and her buddies in its wake. On some days, Nic could still hear the attack play out in her head. Afghanistan had left so many demons behind that she wondered how Rod had dealt with it all plus his injuries. By the looks of it, not well. Not well indeed.

"Can I see him, Doctor?"

⚶⚶⚶⚶

Nic couldn't help but wonder if this was the best place for Rod. She and the doctor walked past a woman shuffling back and forth in a small room, the door wide open so she could be observed, Nic was sure. She looked into what she assumed was the TV room. The sound was turned down low and several people littered the couches, their empty eyes causing Nic to wonder if there was anyone inside, the blank stares directed at them as they passed but didn't seem to register their presence all the same.

The doctor stopped at a room with a dim light barely reaching the door.

"Mr. White, are you up for a visitor?"

The stark room had only a bed in it and a light

hardwired on the wall. Rod was lying on his side facing away from them. The mound didn't move.

"Mr. White—"

"Rod, it's Colonel Caldwell."

"Colonel?" A soft whisper barely audible came out from the bundle of blankets.

"Yes, Rod." Nic walked around the bed and knelt. Nic moved in and rubbed Rod's shoulder. "How are you?"

"I'm sorry." Tears fell. His eyes were swollen and red. He'd been crying a while, she was sure.

"It's okay. We're going to get you some help, buddy."

"Melody?"

"She's fine. Claire, my wife, is with her."

"The baby?"

"He's fine, too."

The doctor's intense gaze as he leaned against the doorframe watching them intently made Nic uncomfortable.

"Doctor, do you mind if I talk to Rod alone?"

"It's not usually allowed, Colonel."

"I'm not going to sneak him out, Doc, I would just like to talk to Rod in private."

"Ten minutes. Fifteen at the most, Colonel."

"Thank you."

Nic waited to speak until the doctor had finally exited the room.

"What happened, Rod?"

Tears squeezed through Rod's tightly shut eyes. He sucked in a deep breath and struggled to sit upright. Nic tried to help, but he pushed her hands away.

"I got this, Colonel." Rod tucked the blanket around his leg with his one good arm.

"Do you mind if I sit down?"

Rod pointed to the foot of his bed and nodded. "Sure."

They sat in companionable silence as Nic waited for Rod to take the lead. She'd asked him twice already, and she didn't want to seem pushy.

"Melody seems like a really nice gal."

Rod nodded. "She is," he whispered and sniffed. "She probably hates me now."

"She doesn't hate you, Rod. She's confused, she's worried, and she's scared."

"Did she say that?"

"Not in so many words. But she wanted me to tell you that she loves you."

Rod cried harder, his body shaking as his head bobbed up and down.

Nic reached over and stroked his leg. "I don't know what happened, buddy, but I'm here for you."

"Can I ask you a question, Colonel?" He looked down at his hand on the blanket, but he didn't look at her.

"Sure. You can ask me anything."

"Have you ever thought that maybe Claire and your daughter would be better off without you here?"

"Are you asking me if I thought I should walk out of their lives?"

"Sorta." He finally looked up at her. The pain in his eyes was palpable. Nic's heart wrenched. What person on earth could say they had never contemplated suicide? Heck, she suspected every puberty-laden girl had at least thought about it. She did when she was coming out and her father ostracized her for almost a year. He even went as far as telling her that she was an abomination to god and that she should kill herself and save her family from the shame of her being a lesbian. The power of someone like a parent telling you to kill yourself could be overwhelming, and a steady word diet of *You should just kill yourself* eventually could become an inevitable outcome instead of a suggestion. Her father was a bully; she didn't need to listen to the girls at school who taunted her because she had her own personal tormentor living under her own roof. Thank god her mother hadn't disowned her, or her senior year in high school would have ended badly for her. While her mother would never take on her father, she had quietly shared Nic's shame, and come to her room and cried with her.

"I don't think Melody agrees with you, Rod. At least that's not the impression I got tonight."

"Hmm." He wiped his nose with the back of his hand. "Colonel...you've been injured. I know you're still going through some health issues. Have they ever gotten to the point where you just think it would be easier if you were dead?"

"Rod...I can't compare what I'm going through with the things you've had to endure—the surgeries, the constant pain—but you've also had some amazing triumphs, too. I'll never be a parent like you. I'll never know what it feels like to have a little me running around."

"Maybe that's what makes this all the more tragic."

Nic was shocked by his statement. How could having a child, marrying the love of your life, and facing a future filled with promise be tragic?

"Tragic? How so?"

"My son is going to have me for a father." He ran his hand down his body. "This broken, messed up, dad.

Would you be proud to have me sitting in the stands when you play baseball? I can't take him hunting or fishing. I can't dance with my wife at our wedding. I'm barely a man as it is, Colonel."

"Wow, I'm not sure where this is coming from, Rod, but I don't see you like that at all. I think you are probably one of the most amazing, giving human beings I have ever met. You have the biggest heart. You work to help others through the support group—"

"Could you take over group? I can't be there right now, and I don't want to let them down."

Her take over group? No way. Didn't he remember she'd quit the group? Hadn't she explained how she wasn't getting anything from group? She hated Mr. Overshare. *Oh, god.*

"I don't know, Rod. I think you're a much better group facilitator. They respect you and you're so conscientious with them. I'm just not you."

"I see." He sighed.

"Rod, what happened tonight?' Time was ticking as Nic noticed the doctor walk past the door for the third time. Every time he passed he was looking down at his watch. He needed to work on the subtlety of his "subtle cues."

Rod finally looked up at Nic. "I called my dad."

Shit. That explained a lot. The same dad that thought Rod would have been better off dead, dad? Rod had wanted to try to win back his father's admiration with the news of a grandson. She was guessing that news wasn't met with great joy.

"Is that why you did this?" Nic was starting to put two and two together. "If I'm not being too nosy, can I ask what he said that would make you want to end it all and leave Melody alone to raise your son?'

Another deep sigh from Rod. He struggled to string together a few words between sobs.

"I've…disappointed you…too…haven't I?"

"Not at all. Is that what your father said, that you were a disappointment?"

Rod nodded.

"Rod…" She rubbed his leg. "He doesn't see how lucky he is to have a son like you, Rod. You're a fucking hero. You saved the lives of your men. I don't know anyone else who would have sacrificed their life for others like you did. You threw yourself on a fucking bomb."

"I guess my dad doesn't see it that way."

"So, what way does your father see it?"

"My brother just got accepted to OCS. He's following in my father's footsteps. He's done everything my father told me to do."

Officer Candidate School was a program in the military that took enlisted soldiers and turned them into commissioned officers. The soldier's knowledge and skill set were an asset, and was often times someone in a servicemember's chain of command recommended them for OCS.

"I see."

"He's sorta the golden boy."

"And your father told you…" Nic couldn't complete the sentence. How could a father be so callous, so insensitive?

"I should just kill myself and save my son the embarrassment of having a father like me."

"Can I tell you something that I've never shared with anyone?" Nic needed to make Rod understand that he had so much more to offer, that his father was just noise that he eventually needed to decide whether to listen to or not.

"Sure."

"When I was just a wee lass." She put her hand down about a foot above the ground and then moved it way up. "Okay, I was in high school. I knew that I liked girls. I never wanted to date boys and I was a bit of a tomboy. Okay, a lot of a tomboy." She smiled and then started again. "The summer before I started my senior year in high school I went to a summer church camp. It was there that I met Susan De Silva. She was cute in a nerdy sorta way. She liked to read a lot and wasn't into sports, but at church camp there isn't reading time except maybe to read the Bible. However, there were lots of sports: swimming, softball, disc golf, square dancing, Capture The Flag. Anyway, I noticed that no one would pick Susan for their teams, she wasn't athletic at all. So, when I was team captain, I picked her first."

"That sounds just like you, Colonel."

Nic smiled and shrugged. "What can I say? I like the underdogs. Anyway, we started hanging out in the dining hall, eating together, sitting next to each other at the campfire where each cabin would do skits. You know, camp-type stuff."

Rod nodded. "Never been to camp so I have no idea, but I'm going to trust you on this."

"Good. Try and stay with me." Nic knew she was making light of the story, but she knew the ending would resonate with Rod. "As the week went on, I realized that I wanted to hold her hand. I thought maybe that I even wanted to kiss her. This was a strange feeling, because I'd never felt that way about guys. I mean, all my friends talked about guys and how handsome they were, and how they wanted to date them. Not me."

Nic paused. She wanted to gather herself before she spilled all the beans.

"And then what happened?"

"We were walking back to our cabins. The rest of the girls were ahead of us and Susan looked over at me and said, 'Have you ever thought about girls, like…you know, how you think about guys?' I didn't know what to say. Of course, I'd been thinking the same thing, too. Anyway, I'll just cut to the chase. I came home from camp knowing I was different."

Nic took a deep breath. "I thought my parents were open-minded. I saw them fight for people who didn't look like us—people of color, the homeless—so I was pretty confident my folks would guide me down this new path my life was going down. Wrong."

"Oh, no."

Nic raised her eyebrows and nodded. "Yep. I told my dad. He was my dad, he taught me how to ride a bike, throw a baseball. We went fishing, did dad stuff. So, I wasn't prepared for his reaction when I told him."

"What did he do?" Rod was leaning into the conversation.

"He told me to…that…um…" Nic choked back the tears and tried to compose herself. "That I should hang myself." She swallowed back the knot that had lodged itself in her throat. "So, sometime parents can be the cruelest of all bullies."

"What did you say?"

"I couldn't say anything. I was devastated. Here was a man I put on a pedestal. He was my dad, man." Nic blinked back the tears as she continued. "I felt like someone had punched me in the gut."

"What about your mom?"

"I loved my mom. We cried together. She begged

me not to listen to my dad, not to do anything even close to killing myself."

"Wow. I can't even imagine telling my son to kill himself."

"No, I can't imagine you would ever say that to anyone, Rod. Is that what your father said to you?"

He looked away from Nic and started to cry again. Nic scooted up the bed and wrapped her arms around him, and they cried together over the loss of their respective fathers. It wasn't just hard to lose a parent that was still alive, it was hard to lose that role model that formed so much of who you were.

"It's okay, buddy. I get it, I really do."

"What did you do with your dad?"

"I cut him out of my life."

"You did?"

"I did. Once I got a scholarship to college, I cut all ties with him. I couldn't have someone like that in my life. It was too toxic."

"I can't believe my dad told me that my son would be better off without me."

"I'm sorry, Rod. I really am. But sometimes we have to cut people out of our lives who aren't good for us, especially if they can't be supportive of us and our families. Melody, your son, they deserve to have you in their lives, Rod. I can't tell you what to do and I would never overstep like that, but I don't want to see you hurting like this."

"Thanks, Colonel. I really appreciate you sharing your story with me."

"This is just between you and me, okay? I've never told Claire about this. I will at some point, but just not now."

Rod raised his hand and crossed his heart. "I

promise she won't hear it from me, Colonel."

"Colonel Caldwell, your time is up." Dr. Tishman tapped his watch. "Rod, I'm going to walk the colonel out and I'll be right back."

Nic grabbed Rod's shoulder as she stood. "You got this, buddy. Any message you want me to give Melody?"

Rod teared up. "Yeah. Tell her I'm sorry and that I love her." He sniffed.

"You got it. Call me if you need me. If I don't hear from you soon, I'll be ringing you, okay?" She raised her fist and he bumped it with his.

"Thanks, thanks a lot. I can't tell you how much your visit means to me, Colonel."

Nic walked down the hallway in silence with the doctor. Just as they reached his office, he said, "That was a doozy of a story you told Rod back there."

Nic gave the doctor a puzzled look. "You think I made it up?"

"Well, let's just say it was quite compelling." He pulled off his glasses and wiped at the lens with a corner of his shirt. "I often see people who try to commiserate by telling stories even more grandiose than what happened to the patient to make them feel like they aren't alone."

"It was quite compelling because it's true."

"If you say so. Looked awfully convenient to me."

"Then I think you should keep wiping at those glasses, sir. I'm not sure how you think you can help people with that crappy outlook. Then again, maybe you're confusing me with one of your patients. I'm not crying out for help here, Doctor, and I'm going to use that term lightly. I'll be checking on Rod tomorrow and if his outlook is worse, I'm going to be knocking on your door."

"I wouldn't make any assumptions that you'll be able to see Rod tomorrow, Colonel. He needs rest to process what he's done and deal with it."

Nic pulled on the handle of the door. "I see. Well, let me say this. If I need to get a lawyer to help Rod out or bring in a second opinion, I will. By the way, I'm sure that your eavesdropping is unethical at best."

"What happens in here, Colonel Caldwell, stays here. Have a nice evening."

The doctor practically hit Nic in the face with the door as he pushed it closed.

Nic gritted her teeth, trying to stop from saying something she would regret later. Her hands clenched into fists and she punched the large automatic door button with her fist.

"Asshole."

Chapter Twelve

Claire handed Melody a cup of tea and then sat next to her. "When are you due?"

"Oh, I'm four months pregnant. In my second trimester."

Melody seemed so young to be pregnant. Then again, when she looked back at her own pictures, which there were few of, she was young herself. Too young.

"Have you picked out names yet?"

"Rod says it's up to me. He doesn't really want our son named after him. Thinks it might be bad luck." Melody blew on her tea.

"Nonsense. It is a bit traditional, but I think Rod is a fine name. If you were thinking of naming him that, of course."

Silence split the tension as Claire looked for something to talk about. The stack of textbooks and spiral-bound notebooks caught her attention. "So, who's the student?"

"Oh, me. I'm studying nursing at CSUMB."

"Me, too."

"Really?"

"Well, not nursing, but I'm in the teacher's program at CSUMB. I just started so I have a ways to go."

"How do you manage it with a kid?"

"Well, it's a challenge. Grace—that's my daughter's name—she's seven, so she's in school. I go to classes while she's in school, and then I do my homework when she's in bed. How far along are you in the nursing program?"

"Only one more semester to go." Melody rolled her eyes and rubbed her stomach again. "I can't wait."

"I'm impressed. I couldn't do nursing. Blood and all…" Claire grimaced. "Yuck. Just not my cup of tea."

Melody laughed. "Yeah, it's not everyone's."

"Do you mind if I ask why nursing?"

"Rod."

"I don't follow. You mean he told you to go to nursing school?"

"Oh, no. He would never tell me what to do. When he got back from deployment, he needed so much care and help with his recovery from all the surgeries. I practically lived at the hospital and I was really impressed with the nurses who took care of him. They were amazing."

Claire nodded as she remembered Nic's time at Walter Reed. The nursing staff had taken great care of Nic as well as helped Claire keep it together.

"So, you and Rod have been together—"

"Since high school. We were high school sweethearts."

"Wow, that's great."

"I thought so, too, but…"

"Look, I don't know what happened tonight to make him do what he did, but…" Claire didn't know what to follow that up with to explain or rationalize what Rod had tried to do. She didn't have the answer, but maybe Melody did. "Do you know why he would do that?"

"All I know was he was going to call his dad and tell him the good news about having a son. He was so excited, and I tried to tell him…" She wiped at the tears streaming down her face again.

"Tell him what?"

"His dad is abusive to Rod—he always has been. When we were in high school, he would come to school with belt marks on his back and arms. Rod could never live up to his father's expectations. That's why he went into the Army. His dad was Army and Rod wanted his dad to be proud of him. He just never was. Now Rod's brother, he could never do wrong."

"I'm so sorry, Melody."

"I keep trying to convince Rod to let him go, but he just keeps trying, and now this…"

"So, we probably shouldn't call his father and let him know what happened. What about his mother? Maybe she should come and support Rod?"

Melody grabbed Claire's forearms and squeezed. Her face was a mosaic of panic.

"No, please don't—she'll tell his father. I don't see how she could come out and not tell his dad. It'll be bad for Rod. You just don't know his father."

Claire's heart ached at the pleading words. How could a parent be so awful to their child? The more she learned about other people's parents the more she realized it was basically a crapshoot on the parent bell curve. Her own father lay somewhere on the middle of the curve with his apology tour now that he had a granddaughter, but that had been Nic's doing. Nic had laid down the law in a long phone conversation just before she left for Afghanistan. It was a no-nonsense, "This is the way it is" conversation, with shades of "If you ever want to see your granddaughter, you'll play nice in the sand box." He later told Claire he respected Nic's protective attitude and clear and direct approach, and on the sly said he liked her better than her ex-husband Mike.

"I won't. It's okay," Claire said as she wrapped Melody in a hug. "It's going to be okay. I promise. What about your parents? Should we call them? I don't think you should be alone tonight."

Melody shook her head. "I'll be okay. I don't want to call them until we know what's going on with Rod. Do you think they'll let me see him?"

"I'm not sure. I'm hoping Nic will have some answers when she gets back."

They both looked at the ornate cuckoo clock on the wall. Claire had seen them before on lots of Army families' walls. It usually meant someone had done a tour in Germany, home of the Black Forest cuckoo clocks.

"Germany?"

"How did you know?"

Claire smiled. "Just a good guess."

"Just after Rod got out of his Advanced Individual Training after Basic, we got stationed in Germany for three quick years. It was the best time of my life. I'd never been out of the States. We were newly engaged, and we took every opportunity to see Europe. Mostly trips through the Morale Welfare and Recreation office, but they were fun and filled with couples from his unit. Then home to the States for a tour, then he was shipped overseas to Iraq."

"Sounds like great fun."

"It was. Then he came home from Iraq, literally half a man."

"I'm so sorry."

"It's okay. He might have come back with fewer parts, but the man who finally rolled through that door was ten times a better man than the one who left."

"What do you mean?" Claire was confused.

"Rod was just like his dad in a lot of ways. He was always pushing himself to be better, faster, and do more just to show his dad he was worthy of his love. When he came back, he was different—calm, more loving. His attitude about life had done a one-eighty."

"Ah, I see."

"I wouldn't go back to the old Rod even if it meant he kept all his parts. I know it sounds selfish, but I really love this Rod."

"It doesn't sound selfish at all."

Headlight beams lit up the living room.

Claire looked down at her watch. Nic had been gone a long time. "That must be Nic. I'll go get her and maybe we can finally get some information about Rod."

"Thanks," Melody said.

Claire hoped Nic had something positive for Melody.

⁂

Nic pulled up to Rod's house. What would she say to Melody? Rod had done something he would regret later. It wasn't a sign of weakness, at least not in Nic's mind. It was the kind of brainwashing cult leaders did to followers. That constant drum beat of *You just don't measure up* and *You should just kill yourself* was noise you heard in your brain even when you slept.

Bang.

Bang.

Bang went the drum.

Nic jumped when Claire tapped on the window.

Opening the door, she scoped Claire up in her arms and buried her nose in Claire's familiar scent.

"That bad, huh?"

"Sorta."

"How's he doing?"

"Okay. Let's go inside so I can give Melody an update."

Claire held Nic in place. "Hold on. I need to tell you that Melody doesn't want Rod's family to know what happened."

Nic nodded in agreement. "Yeah. I got a really good sense of what an asshole Rod's dad is."

Claire threaded her arm through Nic's and walked with her toward the house. A car pulled up to the curb, and a woman rolled the window down. "Hey, is Melody all right?"

Claire bent down to look at the woman. "Who wants to know?" Nic was proud of Claire for being instinctually protective. Then again, it was in Claire's inherent nature.

"Oh, sorry." The woman extended her hand out of the window. "I'm her best friend, Misha. I got a call from someone that something happened, but they didn't know the details. I've been trying to call her, but it keeps going to voicemail. So, I thought I'd take a chance and drive over."

"She's okay, but I'm not sure she's up for company. But I can go in and ask if you want."

"Gosh, no. I don't want to impose. Can you just tell her I came by? And that if she needs me, I'll be over in a heartbeat."

"I'm Claire, by the way."

"Hi, Claire."

"Okay, I'll tell her. I'm sure she'll want to see

you. I think it's just a little hard. In fact, we're getting ready to go home in a few, so I'll tell her to call you. Do you think you can come over and spend the night if she needs you?"

"I'll go home and pack a bag right now. Tell her to call me when she's ready. I don't live far." She moved her hand in a circular motion. Nic was sure it meant something to Misha, but for them, nothing.

"Okay."

"Okay, bye."

"Maybe I should have told her to go in and talk to Melody."

"Well, let me talk to Melody first and then we can decide what to do."

"I don't think she should be alone, Nic."

"No, I agree. I just don't want there to be an audience when I talk to her about Rod."

"Is it that bad?"

Nic sighed. "I'd like to think he's going to be okay with some counseling. How's Melody?"

"Worried." Claire pulled Nic to a stop. "Please tell me that no matter how bad things get, you'll never contemplate suicide as an option."

Nic's heart melted. She'd read the articles that said suicide spurred others to contemplate it, but she wasn't the one to worry about. Nic was worried about those people in group who thought Rod had his shit together.

Nic cupped Claire's face in her hands and bent down and kissed her. Resting her forehead on Claire's, she said, "I would never. No matter how bad the migraines get, I will never think that suicide is a way out. I would never do that to you and Grace. I love you both too much to do that to your lives."

Claire kissed her again, the taste of desperation on her lips. "I love you."

"I love you, too."

"I'm sure Melody's wondering what's going on. Let's get this over with and we can go home."

Chapter Thirteen

Cece sat at the small table in the coffee shop writing up her report on the suicide attempt tonight.

"Geez, did you see that guy? Half of the dude was missing," Murdoch said, setting a coffee cup on the table. "Here, I figure you could use this after that shit tonight."

Cece picked up the cup and took a sip. "Thanks." She tipped it in his direction.

"What'd ya think happened to him? I think I'd want to kill myself, too, if I had to look forward to living the rest of my life like that. Wow." Murdoch leaned back in his chair and stuffed his hands into his ballistic vest. Cece wanted to tell Murdoch what a jerk he was, but she was also aware that being part of such a small department had its limitations for upward mobility. He was her commanding officer, and as such she had to respect the rank. She kept her mouth shut.

"Did the dude say anything to you?"

"No. He wasn't exactly in any shape to say anything."

"So, you knew the woman he referenced in the note, huh?"

"Yeah. We served together over in Afghanistan. She's one of the reasons I decided to come up to Monterey."

"Huh. What branch?"

"Marines."

"No kidding."

"Yep, we were both in the bombing over in Afghanistan." Cece kept writing.

"Hmm. Was that her wife?"

"At the house?"

"Yeah. I assume she's gay."

"LT, where are you going with this? She doesn't live on campus, so we won't see her again."

"Just making conversation, Ramirez. Just making conversation." He tipped forward, grabbed his coffee, and walked out of the coffee shop.

Great, she thought. Now she'd pissed off someone who could make her life miserable and she'd only been on the job a short time. Packing up her stuff, she walked outside and got in the car.

"So, you find a place to live yet?"

Maybe he wasn't as pissed as she thought.

"Yeah, I rented a townhouse in Marina."

"Cool. I'm sure it will be great to have your family up here with you."

Now, she really was worried. He had been hard to read since they'd been riding together for the last few weeks, but now that she would be on patrol on her own, she wondered where he was going with all of this sudden niceness.

"Yeah, I miss my daughter."

"I bet. Hey, I'm starving." He pulled into the drive-through of a burger joint off campus. "I'm buying, what do you want?"

"I can buy my own dinner. Thanks anyway."

She wanted to keep a clean set of boundaries with Murdoch. She didn't want to owe anyone, and the fact that he had bought her coffee tonight was as far as she wanted to let it go. Blurring the lines between work and friendship never worked out. While there was a blue code, she wasn't quite sure she wanted to hang out with someone like Murdoch who clearly had some issues with the students. She was sure he thought they had a connection because of their Army service and now both being cops together.

"So, you won't let me take you to dinner, huh? I see."

Cece flashed him a look of surprise. *Did he just go there?*

He put up his hands. "Hey, I was just kidding. Calm down, I can see it all over your face."

What did someone say to something like that? She knew there was one other female on the force, but she hadn't had a chance to talk to her. She worked the other shift, but now she would make it a point to talk to her and get her perspective on the department.

"I'm good. Let's not talk like that, okay? I should probably tell you that I don't date people I work with. I like to keep clean boundary lines."

Murdoch moved up the line in the drive-through, then looked at her. "Hey, wow. Not even going there. I was just joking."

"I was just letting you know. In case you were wondering."

"Good to know, Ramirez. Good to know."

⁂

Nic sat with Melody on the couch, Claire sat off to the side. Nic was ready for the night to end, to go home and cuddle with her wife and forget today, but she needed to get this over with first.

"How's Rod doing?"

"Well, I finally got a chance to see him. He's okay. Do you know why he did this, Melody?"

"I suspect it had something to do with his father. Rod's father rides him a lot. He's not a very nice man. I was telling Claire earlier that he was very abusive to Rod when we were growing up and that's just continued to now. He talks awful to Rod. I've told Rod not to talk to him, but he…" Melody wiped at her nose.

Nic rested her hand on Melody's leg, trying to offer some reassurance. "I kinda got a sense of that when I spoke with Rod."

"What else did he say?"

Nic looked at Claire, knowing what she was about to say might surprise them all. She bit the inside of her lip nervously.

"Colonel, you can tell me anything. Rod and I don't have any secrets. At least I hope we don't." She rested her hand on Nic's.

"I asked Rod if I could share our conversation. He said he didn't mind but that he wanted you to know how much he loves you first."

"Okay."

"I guess it all started with the phone call to his dad. He was excited about the news of the baby being a boy and he thought his father would be proud to know he was having a grandson. That couldn't have been further from the truth." Nic took a deep breath and continued. "I guess his dad wasn't excited at all, and instead asked him how he could be so selfish to bring a son into this world in his condition. I guess they argued, and his dad said he should just kill himself and be done with it."

Melody sucked in a breath, her hand covering

her mouth. Claire had the same shocked look on her face.

Family: the friends you couldn't choose, but the enemy that often lived within.

Isabella

Chapter Fourteen

Nic had called Cece to have lunch to discuss Rod, group, and to see how the move was going. A chest bump and half hug was the only way Nic knew how to greet another strong woman. Okay, that may not be true, but it seemed appropriate for Cece. With so few friends around she was sure Claire was getting sick of seeing her around the house.

"Hey." Cece slipped into the booth and tossed her hat on the seat. "How are you and the fam doing?"

"Good. How about you? You seem rather chipper today."

Cece offered her a toothy grin. "I am happy. I think I've found a place, finally. I put a deposit on it, I just need to get the keys and then drive down and get my family."

"Hey, that's great, buddy. Do you need some help moving?" Nic was excited for Cece. It was hard being away from family; she hated it when she was shipped overseas. Early in her career, each time she was shipped out her girlfriend left, always saying something about being all alone with no one to depend on. How she got lucky to connect with Claire was beyond her. Independent, smart, beautiful—she had a laundry list of great qualities and only a few things she wasn't thrilled about. Heck, they weren't even issues; they were merely light annoyances, and that only when she was in a bad mood.

On second thought, there was Jordan. Claire's friend Jordan could get on her nerves, but only because Jordan liked to poke at her. She smiled. She really couldn't hold Jordan up as a ding against Claire. Over time she'd even become used to Jordan's overprotectiveness when it came to Claire.

"What are you smiling about?" Cece motioned for the waitress.

"Nothing." Nic opened the menu, closed her eyes and made a swirling motion, stopped, and dropped her finger on an item.

"Interesting way to pick out your lunch," Cece said over her menu.

"I like to be surprised. Besides, if there was something on the menu I didn't like, I wouldn't risk it."

"What'll you girls have?" The waitress was right out of a fifties' diner. The only things missing were the white shoes and the cotton-candy-colored dress, but she was all attitude.

"I'll have the…What are you having, Nic?"

"I'm having the super melt with fries and a chocolate shake."

"Sounds good. I'll have that, too."

"Would you like something else to drink?"

"Oh, yeah." Cece swirled her finger and landed on the menu. "Cool, lemonade." She handed the menus off and laughed.

"What's so funny?"

"I hate lemonade."

"Then why did you get it, silly?"

"Live dangerously."

"If that's living dangerously, sign me up." Nic leaned back and stretched her arms across the red

Naugahyde.

"You want to talk about Rod?" Cece added some sugar to her lemonade.

"Not sweet enough, huh?"

Cece squinted one eye and grimaced just like Grace did when she sucked on a lemon.

"It's good. I'm not sure what Lita sees in it, but it's not bad." Cece added more sugar. "Why are you dodging my question, Nic?"

"I'm not. I did call to have lunch and to talk shop."

"Shop for me, but not for you?"

"Yeah." Nic stirred her milkshake to loosen it up. "Rod asked me to take over group until he can come back."

"How do you feel about that?"

"I hate it."

"Why?"

"'Cause some of those people are just…I don't know. I quit group cause I'm not one to share my shit. Yet some of those guys, they just can't get enough attention or something."

"Aren't you being just a bit judgy? I mean you have a lot in common with them whether you want to admit it or not."

Nic stretched her neck and looked up at the ceiling.

"You aren't going to find the answers up there, Nic. You know what your heart is telling you, right?"

Nic wiggled in her seat and made a face at Cece. "Yes, yes I know what the right thing to do is. But I really don't want to do it." Nic looked around the diner and wondered about the people sitting around her. They all had stories to tell, too. Did they all need counseling, or were they coasting through life like her and Cece?

"Do you ever wonder what everyone's story is, Cece?"

"What do you mean?"

"I noticed you sit with your back to the wall. You're always on alert. You watch people coming in and going out."

"Well, you're very observant yourself, Nic. I didn't know you paid attention to people, too."

"I think it's a product of being in Afghanistan. That guy who killed everyone in headquarters, the bombing." Nic pointed to her face. The scar, while faded, was still a constant reminder of Afghanistan. "I feel like I need to be on alert."

"You mean like those two guys at the Patel market."

"Yeah, just like that. And then I wonder how I could have missed all the signs with Rod."

"Nic, it's not your fault. You couldn't have known what he was going to do. He probably didn't even know he was going to do that until that call." Cece touched Nic's hand and squeezed. "His dad really did a head job on him. Who tells their kid to kill themselves?"

Nic looked at Cece and wondered if she could see her secret, too. She wasn't about to spill her guts again. Once she had dredged up enough bad memories that night with Rod, all she could do was go home and ask Claire to hold her and promise to never let her lose her shit like that, ever. What a burden she'd placed on her wife. She'd apologized the next morning, but Claire had said she understood.

"Yeah. It's tough to have parents like that."

"No shit."

Both women kept silent while the waitress placed their order on the table. Reaching for the ketchup, Nic smacked the bottom of the bottle and looked inside. She jabbed her knife into the bottle and smacked it on the bottom again, forcing a blob onto the table.

"Smooth, Nic."

"It's one of my many skills."

Grabbing the bottle, Cece tapped the side and watched as the ketchup slowly oozed onto her plate. "That is a skill. So, whatever happened to those two little shits who hassled the Patels?"

"I heard from Colonel Tower and she said they are giving them a reduction in rank and a discharge."

"Seriously?"

"Well, Sinclar is getting a general discharge. As for Moffett, I'm not quite sure what's happening there. I was told he is fighting it, so that could be something that prolongs the discharge. Either way, not having an honorable discharge isn't a good thing. At least they didn't get a dishonorable discharge. That would be bad."

"No shit. And after their conduct, they are lucky bastards it's not dishonorable." Cece stuffed a few fries in her mouth. Nic wondered why the change in attitude on Tower's part, but it wasn't her fight. She'd reported the incident and she didn't have time to over think it. It was above her pay grade.

"I heard the captain got a letter or something in his file. Seems he knew about their prior bad behavior and didn't do anything, even on the advice of his staff sergeant."

"Oh." She wagged a fry at Nic. "That's never a good sign. A non-commissioned officer needs to know that the leadership has his back." Cece grimaced.

Nic nodded. The worst thing that could happen in a unit was leadership that didn't work together. "Do you miss it?"

"Naw, I did my time. I got a portion of my retirement, so I'm good. Besides, that part of my life is over and I'm ready to grab onto the next part, start fresh, and be with my family."

"I get it."

"So, you wanna talk about what happened with Rod? How's he doing?"

"Good. He's home, getting counseling."

"That's good."

"He wants me to take over group."

Cece kept her head down but looked sideways at Nic. "Yeah, you said that before, but you never said you would. Are you sure you wanna do that?"

Leaning back against the seat, Nic rubbed her chin. She really wasn't sure she wanted to, but Rod had asked as a personal favor. How could she turn him down in his hour of need? He'd said it would only be for a few sessions until the counselor cleared him to be back.

"He asked me to do him a solid. How could I tell him no?"

"Hmm. You got a million bucks?"

Nic laughed. "No, why?"

"Well, since you are doling out favors. I thought I'd ask."

"Ha, ha. I'm really torn here."

"I can see that. Look it's for a short time, right? So consider it your good deed for the year. Besides, you're a great role model." Shoving another fry in her mouth, she talked around it. "When do you start?"

"End of the week."

"What does Claire think?"

Nic shrugged. "She thinks it would be a good idea. She knows I hated group. All that oversharing stuff just isn't my style. She thinks if I go as a leader, maybe I can get something out of it by helping others."

"She's probably right."

Nic sighed. "She always is."

"Want me to come?"

"Would you?"

"Nope, just wanted to put that out there."

"You're a real shit, you know that?"

"Yep. That's what my mom says."

"That's not why I called you."

Cece shot her a surprised look. "Okay."

"I might just be paranoid, but I've been seeing the same car parked in my neighborhood, at the store, on campus—different places. It's like I have my head on a swivel, sorta like when we were in Afghanistan, but not so general. I'm constantly on alert. I know that's not new, but this seems like there's a real threat, a specific one."

"Got a make, model, and plate for it? Or a description of the driver?"

"Yeah, but look, I'm not going to ask you to run the stuff. I don't want to compromise your job."

"Then you need to go down and file a report with the police, Nic."

"Yeah, I know, I know."

"Promise me you will." Nic could see Cece was dead serious now. No more joking, no more fun and games. Stalking was a serious business, and with the recent events and Nic being a lesbian…Sometimes it worked out to be nothing but she was sure Cece didn't believe in coincidence. Cece glared at Nic when she didn't respond.

"Okay, okay, I will."

"Have you told Claire?"

"What? No, I don't want her to worry. It's bad enough I'm making a big deal out of what's probably nothing. I'm sure it's probably related to my PTSD."

"Go with your gut, Nic. You know when something is off." Cece took another sip of her lemonade and winced. "Yeah, I'm not getting that again."

"Serves you right, sourpuss." Nic clinked her glass against Cece's.

Nic knew Cece was right: go with her gut. Something wasn't right.

⁂ ⁂ ⁂ ⁂

Nic had been acting strange since Rod's suicide attempt. She'd been leading group for the last few sessions and each time she came back edgy, tired, and a little distant. Actually, a lot distant. The group met again tonight and Claire wanted to speak to Nic before she left to try to get to the bottom of the mood.

Walking into their bedroom, she found Nic still sitting on the bed in her underwear.

"Sweetheart, you okay?" Claire practically sat right on her as she squeezed next to Nic. She smelled like soap, her favorite kind, too. She ran her finger through the short, wet locks and pushed them off Nic's face. Her finger traced the faint line of a scar and then trailed around Nic's ear. She leaned in and let her tongue tease Nic's ear, knowing it would make her break out in goosebumps at the contact.

"What's wrong?" she whispered.

Nic tugged at the T-shirt in her hand. Dropping

it to the floor, she wrapped her arms around Claire, leaned back, and pulled her on top of her.

"I'm just…" Nic struggled. "I don't know."

Claire pushed herself farther up Nic's body, forcing Nic backward. She slowly rubbed herself against Nic. Nic had a way of just being sexy that didn't take any effort at all, and she was oblivious to the way it affected Claire when Nic walked around half naked. She felt like a newlywed who just couldn't keep her hands off her new wife.

Resting her chin on her hands, she looked down at her lover. "I bet I know what can get you out of this funk." Claire offered her sexiest grin.

Nic tilted her head closer to Claire's. "Do you?"

"Uh-huh."

"Do tell."

"Actually, I have to show you. I don't do tell very well."

"Hmm." Nic smiled.

Claire pushed herself down until her hips were on top of Nic's. She gyrated just enough that she felt Nic's hips buck at the contact. Stopping, she sat up and pulled off her T-shirt and ran her fingers over the lace cups of her bra. Nic's reaction was immediate as she lowered her eyes into the smoldering expression she got when she was turned on. Claire unhooked the front of her bra and let it fall open, then grabbed Nic's hands and placed them on her breasts. She rubbed herself against the palms of Nic's hands and seductively bit her lower lip. She rolled her hips back and forth over Nic as she let out a little moan.

That was it. Nic rolled her over and was on top of Claire in an instant, her mouth covering her mound. She could feel Nic's hot breath through the thin cloth of her yoga pants. Without missing a beat, Nic slid them down and slid her tongue between Claire's folds, hitting her clit. Her body bucked instinctively as she reached down and held Nic's head in place.

"Fuck," she whispered.

"I plan to," Nic said, her tongue going back at Claire's clit. Nic slid her pants farther down her legs and nudged her knees wider.

Closing her eyes, she reveled in the way only Nic could make her feel. The slight chill, the electricity that shot through her body at Nic's touch, all of it made her feel more than alive. It was almost an out-of-body experience at times. Her body contracted as Nic entered her.

The licking, pumping continued, and Claire was on her way to a full-blown orgasm. She held Nic's head and rolled her hips looking for just the right contact to bring her to orgasm again. Goosebumps popped down her legs. Just behind her knees and ankles a sweat broke out, signaling a deep, swelling orgasm.

"Oh."

Nic pushed her harder, and like clockwork Claire bucked her hips from the contact as Nic's lips tensed. As she shook, she watched Nic stalk up her body like a big cat and then gently lay her body down on Claire's.

Claire wrapped her legs around Nic's hips and tensed at the contact. She tried to flip Nic over, but Nic held firm.

"Your turn, lover," she whispered in Nic's ear and kissed her neck.

"I'm good." Nic moved her head, giving Claire better access.

"That's not fair."

"It's fair to me. Besides, I just want to hold you

and show you how much I love you."

"Nic…"

Nic held up her hand and pretended to scowl. "I'm the boss." She laughed and held Claire tight.

Sometimes Nic was on board with being intimate, and sometimes…Well, today wasn't going to be one of those days. Claire had seen a lot of this Nic lately and she wasn't happy about it. It would take time to bring that wall completely down.

"Okay, you're the boss…"

"Good."

"…For now, but I will get my way."

Nic smiled. "You always do, my love. You always do."

Chapter Fifteen

Nic stood in the parking lot leaning against her car. She was stalling for time and she knew it. She was twenty minutes early, but she recognized some of the group members' cars already parked in the lot. A car several rows over caught her eye. The dark blue, late-model Honda with hailstone dents all over it was there in the back. She started to walk over to it but was cut off by Rod's white van.

"Hey, Nic, how are you?"

"Rod? What're you doing here, buddy?"

He smiled the biggest smile she'd seen in a long time.

"My counselor said I could come by group, see everyone, and give them an update."

"That's great." What Nic wanted to say was, *thank God I don't have to do this anymore,* but she didn't. He hadn't said he could take the group back, just that he could come by and say hi. Baby steps, Nic thought.

"Yeah, so give me a minute. I'll park this and we can walk in together."

"Sure."

Nic waited at the back of the van for Rod. It didn't take long for the rear doors to swing open and the ramp to extend to the ground. She was always amazed at the technology that allowed Rod to drive a car without the assistance of another person. It restored his independence to get around without the help of others.

He must have noticed the look of surprise on her face as she caught the first glimpse of his new ride. "Like it?"

"Wow. This is amazing." She walked around what she could only describe as a wheelchair on steroids. It sported huge bloated tires with knobs and a massive frame that looked like it could tackle anything from city streets to the paths at the local county park.

"Where did you get this? It looks like you could go four-wheeling in it."

"I can. It's designed to be able to go on dirt paths, snow, and sand. I can go to the beach!"

"No kidding."

"I saw it on a documentary they did about this disabled vet and how this company designed a power chair that could let him go fishing with his kids. So, I contacted the company and got on a list months ago. I figured since I got a 'guvvy' job now—"

"Wait, you got a job? That's awesome news, buddy." She slapped him on the back. Amazing how a couple of weeks could change a person's life.

"Yeah, once I finish computer school. One of my instructors works for a contractor over on post and told me to fill out the application and he would vouch for me. Seems I'm an Ability One hire and they need all of the Ability Ones they can get. So, bam. I'm getting a job at the DOD annex on base."

Nic grabbed his shoulder and squeezed. Finally something was going right for a change. "That's great news, man." Nic fist-bumped him. "I'm so happy for you." She really was thrilled for the man. "Hey, hold on a second." She held up a finger.

Nic looked back at the Honda and the bad feeling

jumped into her gut again.

Go with your gut, Nic, Cece had said.

Pulling out her phone, she ran over to the car.

Empty.

She snapped a pic of the license plate, a few more of the car, and then looked inside. A coffee cup, a scrunched up empty pack of cigarettes, and a blanket were the only occupants. Nothing stood out to Nic and she felt a little relieved. Except for the blanket on the passenger seat—that was odd. She sent the photos to Cece with a short message.

Off to group and saw this car again. I'll call later. Nic ran back to Rod.

"Everything okay?"

"Yeah, just thought I saw someone I knew. Ready?"

"Yes, ma'am."

The church loomed in front of them as they made their way toward the building. Nic was glad that there was a side entrance. She hated walking through the main church to get to the room in the basement where group was held. The smell was something that always took her back to her childhood and the memories of church every Sunday. Until she came out. Then, her father at one point forbade her to go until she changed her mind about being gay. When that didn't happen, he forced her to go to every service. If there was something happening at the church, he made her go. He figured force-feeding her a steady diet of bible study and worship would cure her of her love for women. He couldn't have been more wrong.

"Hey, watcha thinking about?"

"What? Oh, nothing."

"Hmm, that frown on your face didn't look like

nothing."

"It's my resting bitch face." She laughed and punched him in the shoulder. "At least that's what Claire calls it when she's mad at me."

"Melody calls it my pouty face."

"Pouty, huh?"

There was an eerie silence that didn't sit well with Nic as they walked. Usually the place was bustling with people from the church, parishioners helping clean and do some of the work around the grounds.

"Ah, Nic." Pastor Walton came out of his office. "Rod! Well, son, it's great to see you. I've been praying for you every day."

"Thank you, Pastor. I appreciate that."

"So, have we set a wedding date yet?"

"Not yet, but I'm trying to pin her down. With the baby and graduation all coming so soon, we've kind of had our hands tied."

"Well, don't wait too long. We love weddings around here."

"Where is everyone Pastor Walton?" Nic asked.

"Oh, yes. Well, today's the day we minister to the sick, and for some reason, the flu has really taken its toll. So, it's been quiet. I'm on my way to the hospital myself."

"Are you sick, Pastor?"

"Oh, no, son. I just have to visit Mrs. Myrtle. Fell and broke her hip, poor thing."

"Oh, I'm sorry to hear that."

"Yes, well I'm off. Choir practice starts in an hour, so the rectory will be filled with shouts of 'Hallelujah' soon." He looked down at his watch. "I don't want to be late. Mrs. Myrtle notices stuff like that, you know."

He pushed his boxy glasses back up his nose and

waved. Either Nic was getting old, or everyone around her was still in high school. He just seemed to be too young to be a pastor of a church the size of The Good Shepard.

Nic took a deep breath and watched as Rod took the lead to the elevator. Group was waiting.

"I like Pastor Walton. He's a really nice guy."

"Hmm, he seems very young," Nic said, pushing the Down button.

"You think he's too young?" Rod gave Nic a curious look. "We joined the Army young. Well, I did and you joined the Corps."

"I promise not to hold it against you, Rod. Besides, I never bet on the Army/Navy game."

"Why not?"

"I don't like football, and the Navy guys always gave us a bad time when we went out to the field."

"Ah, I see."

"Probably not, but I'll trust you on that, Rod." Nic laughed as she got out of the elevator and held the door for Rod.

"I've missed our usual banter, Nic."

Rod's new wheelchair took up some sizeable space, and Nic walked behind it rather than trying to dodge the chairs, tables, and other church items that hugged the wall. Walking into the room, she saw everyone sitting in their seats but no one was saying a word. Cookies and punch were laid out on the table, yet Mr. Overshare wasn't stuffing his face. Instead, everyone had their eyes on Nic and Rod.

"Hey, everyone. How are you?" Rod yelled out. When no one said anything, Rod looked at Nic. "Was it something I said?"

"No, it was something I said." A strange male's

voice boomed behind Nic. The sound of a shotgun chambering a round echoed in the room and Nic felt cold steel press the base of her neck. "Good morning, Colonel Caldwell."

Chapter Sixteen

ece looked down at her phone and smiled. Unfortunately, Nic's text message would have to wait until she was finished with the traffic stop.

"Good morning, Officer. I'm so sorry I was speeding. I was on my way to the gym and I'm late." The young woman puffed her chest up, the straps of her shirt barely keeping her breasts from popping out.

"That's okay, ma'am. At least you're honest." Cece lowered her sunglasses to look into the dark interior of the vehicle. The frustration on the woman's face clearly meant she was expecting a male officer, probably someone like Murdoch who certainly would exchange the proffered view for leniency. "License, registration, and proof of insurance, please. Do you live on campus, Miss..." Cece looked at the license. The photo resembled the driver if you got rid of the implants, the red lipstick, and the false eyelashes. Who went to the gym dolled up like that? These days, young people never surprised her, especially college students. In her past life, men and women were squared away and respectful. Kids now were almost like a foreign life force from a different planet.

"Miss Lopez, you look a little different than your license. Would you mind just stepping out of your car so I can make sure it's you?"

"Seriously? Didn't I just tell you I'm late to the gym? My trainer is waiting on me and if I don't get a move on, he's going to leave again."

"Well, the longer you take to exit the vehicle, the more likely your trainer is to leave."

"Oh, my god. I'm calling my dad. What's your name?"

"Cece Ramirez. Badge number three-two-five-eight."

"Ramirez, huh?" The way she rolled her Rs surprised Cece. When she got out of the car, the young woman went all ghetto on her, complete with neck popping and finger snapping. Attitude bounced off her like a cholita. Cece had met lots of girls like her in her South-Central neighborhood. It was the whole reason she'd moved Melita up to Monterey last week.

"Do you know who my father is?" Lopez said pulling down her top.

"Not a clue. Should I?"

"Bitch, please."

Cece put up her hand. "You need to stop right there and back that up. I didn't use that kind of language with you, so show some respect and watch your mouth."

"Are you kidding me right now?"

Cece smiled. For all of her five feet four inches, she clearly wasn't intimidated by Cece looking down at her, or the gun on her hip. Cece just shook her head. This girl reminded Cece of a little dog that didn't know it was small and insignificant in the big dog world.

"Ma'am, I don't kid. So..." Cece sized her up and matched her to her driver's license. "You can get back in the car. I'll be right back."

Before Cece could even turn around and hoof it back to her car to run her information, she heard the young woman on the phone. "Daddy, you are not going to believe what's happening. A stupid cop pulled me over for going like five miles over the speed limit."

Cece scoffed. Five miles would have been a pass. She wouldn't waste her time on something so trivial, but this gal was going twenty miles over the limit down Inter-Garrison Road with her music blaring while texting on her phone. Oh lord, this was starting to be one of those days.

⁂

A cold sweat broke out across Nic's body as she raised her hands up. Her fight-or-flight response amped up. Looking around the room, she saw the frightened eyes of the group staring at her, mouths agape. She confirmed in a sideways glance that Rod was a comfortable distance to her right. She started to turn and felt the muzzle of the shotgun pushed harder against her head.

"Don't even think about it, Colonel."

She still didn't recognize the voice.

"Get on your knees," he yelled.

"I'm not getting on my knees. If you're going to shoot me in the back, you're going to do it while I'm standing."

"Oh, I'm not going to shoot you yet. I want you to suffer like I'm going to suffer for the rest of my life, you fucking dyke."

Now she recognized the voice.

"Lance Corporal Moffett—"

"Not anymore thanks to you, Colonel Dyke." He shoved the barrel against her head with each word.

Nic's jaw clenched as Moffett shoved the shotgun against her head.

"Hey, leave Colonel Caldwell alone," Rod said.

Shit.

"What do you want, gimp? What are you going to do, roll over me with that wheelchair?"

"Rod, don't."

"Yeah, Rod. Shut the fuck up. My beef isn't with you or anyone else in this room, but it could be if anyone gets any great idea about helping the colonel here. Understand?"

"Let them go and I'll stay here with you, Moffett."

"You ain't in any position to make demands, Colonel. As I see it, I'm holding all of the cards. Hey, you?" She couldn't see who he was yelling at until Mr. Overshare pointed to himself. "Yeah, you. Bring me a chair."

Mr. Overshare got up and walked his chair over to Moffett. "Thank you. Get on your knees, Colonel."

"No."

He kicked Nic's right knee and she buckled to the ground, landing on all fours.

"Fucking asshole."

He laughed at her as she stayed down on her hands and knees.

"What did you say?"

"I called you an asshole."

"No, you called me a fucking asshole."

As Nic straightened up, everything went black.

❧❧❧❧

"I'm going to file a complaint with your commander," Lopez yelled at Cece.

"Ma'am, you're more than welcome to speak to my superior. All of this has been recorded on both my body cam and the camera in the squad car. You were going over thirty-five miles an hour in a fifteen zone, you were on your phone, and you didn't have your seat belt on."

"You can't write me up for being on my cell phone."

"California is a hands-free-device state. So, yes, I can write you up for that and no seat belt as well as the speeding."

"I had to undo my seat belt to get my driver's license and registration."

"Ma'am, when I walked up to the car, you weren't wearing your seat belt."

"Daddy, did you hear all of that?"

"Sign the ticket, honey, and let the officer do their job."

"But Daddy," she whined, taking the phone off speaker. "Yes, but…Fine."

Cece grabbed her clipboard before it dropped to the asphalt. "Have a nice day, ma'am."

"Stop calling me 'ma'am.' I'm not old like you." She pulled away, flipping Cece the bird as she sped down the road. She would be happy to give the woman another ticket if that's what she wanted.

Tossing her clipboard on the passenger seat, she pulled out her phone, remembering the text from Nic.

She read the text and tapped on the photos Nic had sent. Something wasn't right. Looking at her watch, she made a mental note of the time of the text. A little over forty minutes had passed since Nic had sent it. According to Nic, group lasted about an hour. She'd give it another fifteen minutes before she texted Nic back. By the time she stopped and ordered her coffee, she could text Nic.

Something niggled at Cece. Looking at the photos again, she wrote down the license plate and called it in to see who owned the vehicle.

"Officer Ramirez, the vehicle is registered to a Charles Moffett."

Why does that name sound familiar?

"Thank you, dispatch. Wants or warrants?"

"No wants or warrants."

"Address?"

"PO Box three-two-three, Monterey, California."

"Ten-four, dispatch."

Waiting in line at the drive-through, Cece racked her brain. The name. She'd heard that name before. What were the names of the two goons that Nic had encountered at the shopette? Instead of waiting to call she'd just text Nic, and when Nic got out of group she could give Nic the info on the car.

Hey, I ran the license plate and the car comes back registered to a Moffett from Monterey. Call me when you get out of group. No red flags on the registration.

"Thank you," Cece said, grabbing the large cup of coffee.

"Have a great day, Officer."

Cece smiled and waved at the young woman at the window. Well, not all hope was lost on the younger generation, she thought as she drove away. Cece looked at her phone and expected a text back from Nic, but nothing had come through. It was 10:20 now and Nic should have been out of group. If Nic was anything she was good at returning a text message, even if it only had a thumbs-up or a smiley face.

Dialing Nic's phone, she waited. It went to voicemail.

"Nic, it's Cece. Just checking in to see if you recognize the name on the car. Call me when you get a chance."

Moffett.

Moffett.

Why did that name sound so familiar? Something wasn't right and she just couldn't shake the feeling. Taking a chance, she made her way to Nic's house and hoped she'd catch Claire before she left for school. Nic had told her that she hadn't discussed the suspicious car with Claire, so what she was about to do would send one of them into a fit. She didn't care; her gut was telling her something was wrong.

She was in luck. Claire's car was still in the driveway. She radioed dispatch and let them know she was off campus, then grabbed her hat and walked up the walk. Before she could even knock, Claire swung the door wide.

"Is something wrong? Did something happen to Rod again?" Claire was frantic.

Cece put her hands up. "Claire, everything's fine. I was just wondering if you could help me out. Nic texted me some pictures of a car—"

"What car?"

"Um, well, she's seen the same car around town lately and was just being cautious. Anyway, she sent me some pictures of the car and license plate before she went into group. I ran the plate and it came back with a name. I think I've heard the name before, but I can't get a hold of Nic to verify it."

"And you're worried."

Cece visibly squirmed a little. "Let's just say I'm erring on the side of caution."

"Who owns the car?"

Cece tapped the pad against her thigh. She'd said this much, no need to hold back now. "I don't recognize the name and it didn't come back with any wants or warrants. It's probably nothing."

"Tell me, Cece." Claire suddenly took on a momma bear persona as she stepped closer to Cece. What was it with women today? Geez.

She flipped open her pad. "Charles Moffett."

"Oh, shit." Claire looked scared and Cece's heart sank.

"What?"

"He's one of the men in that shopette incident."

"Shit. That's where I've heard the name before. Jesus Christ."

"Do you think something's happened?"

"No, I'm sure it's fine. Just a coincidence. I'm sure it's just a coincidence." Who was she trying to convince, Claire or herself? "Where does Nic meet with group? I thought I'd just drive by and make sure everything's okay."

Bullshit. She was worried, but she wasn't going to let Claire know that if she could avoid it.

"Group meets over at The Good Shepard Church on Lincoln."

"Okay. I'll just give her another call and see if she picks up. I'm sure she's busy with everyone wanting to chat after. You know how those things can become a big ol' gabfest afterward."

"I know bullshit when I hear it, Cece. Why don't I come with you?"

Cece waved her off. "You have Grace, and I'm sure it's nothing. I'll drive by and check things out and tell Nic to give you a call." Cece started to step off the porch when Claire grabbed her, her purse on her arm and keys jangling in her hand.

"I'm coming. You can drive me, or I can follow. Totally up to you."

"You follow me. I can't have a civilian in my car without authorization and we don't have time for that, okay?"

"Yep, works for me. Lights and sirens?" Claire ran past Cece to her car.

"No lights and sirens, and don't tailgate. We're going to look pretty stupid when it turns out there's nothing wrong."

"I'll take her out to lunch, if you know what I mean." Claire waved as she jumped in her car.

"I don't want to know what you mean. I'm perfectly fine with thinking lunch is exactly that—lunch," Cece mumbled to herself. She called dispatch and had them put her out to lunch. It was past eleven, so the cover story worked. Her finger hovered over the Lights button. She wanted to get there as quick as possible, but it would be an abuse. It wouldn't be the first time she abused her rank, just not at this job. She groaned and put her hand back on the steering wheel. It would be enough that people, once they noticed her behind them, would turn off on a side street thinking she might give them a ticket. She's seen it time and time again, so she'd take advantage of that fact of human nature and hope it got her there faster legally.

She tapped her voice-to-text feature and dictated a text message to Nic.

"Hey, Nic. I left ya a text earlier, just thought I'd check back and see if you're free for lunch. I got all my stuff moved up here, including Melita and my mom. I figured it would be great to get the girls together for a playdate." She hit Send. Babbling. It was what she did when she was nervous.

"Pick up. Pick up, Colonel."

Isabella

Chapter Seventeen

Nic's wristwatch silently vibrated. It was her link to her phone, and let her know when she got a text or phone call. Thank god she hated the damn thing enough to keep the ringer turned off. She could only wonder what would happen if it had gone off in front of Moffett. He was so unhinged that he had screamed at someone when their appointment reminder alert gave a barely audible ding.

"Fuck," Nic whispered to herself. Everyone in group knew the no-phone rule, but there was always that one rule breaker. And she knew exactly who it was: Mr. Overshare. *Asshole.*

"Put your fucking phones in a pile, right there." He stood in front of each person, getting right in their face until they tossed their phones on the floor. He kicked at the ones that didn't make it to the middle of the circle.

As he made a slow walk around the circle, Nic took the opportunity to tap out a quick text to Cece.

911 no cops.

She tapped the face and put it back to the time. She hoped Cece would understand what she meant. She received a response right away but didn't dare look down as Moffett stood in front of her.

"Colonel Dyke. Where's your phone?" He held out his hand, still pointing the shotgun at her. He was dressed in his desert diggies, ready for war. He wore a sidearm Velcroed to his chest for easy access, had extra ammo clips in his bulletproof battle vest, and a wicked-looking knife sheathed on his belt. He was prepared for a long stay or complete and total annihilation. Probably both, Nic admitted.

"Come on, come on." He wiggled his fingers. "What, do you have some naked pictures of your wife on your phone?" She placed it in his hands and shot him a dirty look. Then he did something she didn't expect: he pocketed it. It was locked, her fingerprint the only way to open it. If he wanted to he could make her open it, but it would take a little diving to get to her text messages, which would give her away.

"Do you all know why I'm here?"

Nic was pushed backward, landing on her ass.

"Because this bitch decided to get in my business. Now." He knelt down and looked right at her. "I'm being drummed out of the Corps, thanks to you." He poked her in the chest and pushed his finger harder.

She didn't flinch. She wasn't going to give him the pleasure of pain. "You got drummed out of the Corps because you're a poor excuse for a soldier. You went into someone's business and were going to steal from the family. Then—"

Nic took the butt of the shotgun to the face. Unfortunately, it was the same side she'd injured in Afghanistan. She fell back and hit her head on the concrete floor. Colors flashed before her eyes and her vision started to tunnel.

"Fuck."

"Hey, you didn't have to do that," Rod said, moving his wheelchair closer to Nic.

"If I want your opinion, gimp, I'll tug your chain. Now back off." Moffett leaned over Rod, menacing.

"Do you know why we meet?" Rod stood his ground. "This is a group for people dealing with PTSD."

Moffett nodded and looked at each one sitting in the circle. "The weak being led by the weak." He pointed his shotgun at Rod. "I get it. You all have 'issues,' and you need to come here and spill your fucking guts so you can go home and not beat your wife and kids. I get it."

He walked over to Nic and kicked her. "Except for this bitch. She's the reason I'm here for *group*," he said with a sneer.

"Look, I'm sure we can help you. We've all been there, been where you are. What's your name?"

Moffett smiled and sat back down in the rickety chair, stretched his legs out, and laid the barrel of the shotgun between his shoes, still pointing at Nic. "You can call me Moffett."

"Well, Mr. Moffett, I'm sure you can understand that a lot of these people are already dealing with some heavy stuff. They don't need something like this to send them over the edge."

"What about you, gimpy? What are you dealing with? Oh, wait..." He waved his hand around. "Let me guess, you were the bomb boy."

"Shut up," someone in the circle said softly.

"Oh, nice. So, you all aren't broken. I figured you were just zombies from too much medication."

Nic sat up. A migraine was building, and she could only hope to keep her focus.

"You." He pointed to one of the newest members of the group. "Get me some of that punch and a couple of cookies."

"Get them yourself, asshole," she said, venom dripping with each word.

She might be small, but she carries a smart mouth. Nic wiped at the blood dripping down her temple. She gently pushed against her cheek and a light pop rewarded her.

"Fuck," she said under her breath. She was going to make him sorry he ever fucked with her. A beating wouldn't be good enough for the asshole. Nic got to her hands and knees again and steadied herself. Her heart was racing, the sounds of vehicles driving by distracting her. *I'm not in Afghanistan, I'm not in Afghanistan,* she chanted over and over in her mind.

She looked over at the group, making eye contact with each person that wasn't looking at Moffett. She wasn't going to be victim of a fucking terrorist any more than when she was stationed overseas. Mr. Overshare and Nic locked eyes. She motioned her head slightly toward Moffett and then looked at the gun at his chest. Mr. Overshare lowered his hand to his side and raised one finger at a time. Nic panicked. She wasn't ready to take him. Not yet.

She shook her head and grimaced, then mouthed, *No.*

He grimaced back at her.

Wait, she mouthed. She held her hands just slightly enough that he nodded. Thank god he wasn't as dense as she thought.

"Hey, I'm the person you want, asshole. Why don't you let the rest of these people go?"

"Why am I not surprised you want to make the supreme sacrifice?" He pouted his lips and walked toward her. His hand ran over her hair and he grabbed a handful, jerking her head back so she was looking up at him. "'Cause I'm the fuckin' boss here, get it? You don't control this situation, I do." She caught herself as he tried to toss her backward.

"Mr. Moffett, how about I get you that punch and cookies?" Rod moved his wheelchair over to the table and started filling a plate. "Do you like chocolate chip, or raisin, or maybe sugar cookies?"

Moffett pointed to another woman in the group. "You. Make a sign that says, 'Group in session, do not disturb' and show it to me." She did as instructed, and he nodded for her to put the sign on the door. "Now close the doors. I'm watching you, so no funny stuff or I start shooting people.

"Cookie man. Just put them all on the plate."

"You got it." Rod wheeled around and made his way to Moffett. "Here you go, not a big selection but—"

Moffett snatched the plate, a few cookies flying off. He took the cup of punch out of the cup holder and swallowed it in one gulp. "Fill it up again."

"You got it."

Nic wondered what Rod was up to, but she was starting to see an opportunity if he kept diverting Moffett's attention.

"So, Colonel Dyke. You ready to die?"

❦❦❦❦

Cece looked at the text and panicked.

911 no cops.

What the heck did that mean? *Shit.*

Pulling up to the church, Cece noticed lots of young people making their way into the building. More shit. Getting out of her car, she waited for Claire.

"Where does group meet, Claire?"

"Have you heard from Nic?"

"Sorta."

"What do you mean, sorta?"

"I got a three-word text from her."

"There. There's her car." Claire pointed to Nic's SUV parked close to Rod's van.

Great. They were both here. Searching the parking lot, Cece pulled up the picture of the car Nic has sent. If she was lucky it was…No such luck. It sat right where Nic had seen it, too. Shielding her eyes, she looked inside the car. She looked at the door handle, then stopped herself from trying it. If he was off his proverbial rocker, he might have booby-trapped the car. She walked to the passenger side where a blanket sat on the seat. Peering through the windshield, she saw a flap for a box of shotgun shells peeking out. No question, he was armed with at least a shotgun.

"Is this the car?" Claire leaned on the windshield and looked inside. "What are you looking for?" She walked around the car and started to reach for the door handle.

"Don't…don't touch that, please. It could be rigged with an explosive device."

Claire jumped back. "Oh, my god, are you kidding?"

"Claire, better safe than sorry. Let's leave this to the experts."

"Have you called them yet? Nic could be in there with a madman. He was pissed, Nic said, when she met with them. Now, he's following her. This isn't good, Cece. She could be in danger."

Cece grabbed Claire and held her arms tight. "Claire, we need to be calm, right now. Nic texted me, '911 no cops.'"

"What does that mean?"

"I don't know. Clearly, no one knows what's going

on because there are people going into the church right now." Cece pointed to the few young people loitering around the front entrance.

"Choir practice."

"How do you know that?"

Claire pointed to the big sign announcing the week's activities at the church.

"Ah, Captain Obvious. Great, that just makes this all the more serious."

"We need to get in there and see what's going on." Claire started walking toward the church.

"Claire, wait up. Let's think about this before we make things worse."

"How could we make them worse? The group is in there with a psycho and you want to wait?"

"No, I want to come up with a plan and see if we can find out what's going on before we call in for backup."

"Okay, Officer Ramirez, what's your plan?" Claire crossed her arms over her chest and stared Cece down.

"I'll go down into the basement and see if I can see where the group is at. I'll assess the situation and call for backup if he's in there. If he's armed, it means he has hostages. Nic's and Rod's cars are still here, so he has at least two."

"Oh god. Oh god." Claire rocked back and forth holding herself.

"Don't panic, and please don't call anyone until we can figure out what the situation is, okay?"

Claire nodded.

"Promise me." Cece knew she should call for backup right away, but without knowing the situation she could just be panicking for nothing. "I'll be right back. Sit in your car and I'll come back and let you know what I find out. Don't call Nic."

"Okay."

"Give me ten minutes. If I'm not back by then you can call PD and tell them what we suspect."

"Okay."

Chapter Eighteen

The room was eerily quiet. The tick of the hands moving on the wall clock was the only sound at one point. A few members of the group were rocking back and forth in their chairs. They weren't the only ones getting agitated. Moffett was pacing around the group of people, looking at his watch and then at the big clock hanging on the wall. Nic could tell they were all starting to get wound tight.

Suddenly, the church organ played a few notes and spooked everyone as a hymn came to life.

Choir practice.

Barely able to see through her swollen left eye, Nic needed some ice as soon as possible to keep the swelling from closing it completely shut. However, time wasn't on her side. Even a bathroom break where she could wash the blood that had dripped down her face would help.

She watched as Moffett checked his watch again and then pulled out his phone and looked at it. Clearly, he was expecting something or someone, but it hadn't come through yet. She wasn't about to wait for Sinclar to join this little soiree and add to the killer dynamic at play. She glanced at Rod, who was trying to talk down one of the group members who was in tears. She sought out each person, but none made eye contact except Mr. Overshare. She would have to take what she could get and hope his bite was just as bad as the bark he put on display at every meeting.

Nic struggled to get to her feet, catching Moffett's attention.

"What do you think you're doing? Sit back down."

"I need to go pee."

"Pee in a cup." He threw a paper cup at her.

"I'm not peeing in a cup." She wobbled as she tried to take a step toward the door.

"Sit the fuck down, Colonel Dyke." He put his hand on her shoulder.

His first mistake. She put her hands up as he pressed the barrel against her neck. He was in a perfect position for…

She turned to her right. Both hands grabbed the barrel of the shotgun. She put her shoulder into his arm, twisting it out of his right hand. She continued spinning around until she hit him with the butt of the shotgun across his face. He pitched forward, landing on his hands and knees, but his right hand dug into his vest and he came up pointing a 9mm Beretta at her.

She had the shotgun pointing at him.

Blood streamed down his face, his right eye covered in it. If he didn't look demonic before, he definitely did now.

"Get out. Everyone get the fuck out now." Nic didn't take her eyes off him as she screamed at everyone. "Now!"

"Colonel—"

"Rod, get the fuck out, now."

The clatter of chairs falling backward and being stepped on in the rush to get out of the room was the only noise that could drown out the choir above them.

"Shut the door, Rod."

She knew that the police had probably already been called by the escaping hostages—at least she hoped so—but then she spotted the pile of phones still on the floor.

Fuck.

"Well, lookie here. We got us a standoff, Colonel."

"Shut up, Moffett. Did you really think I would let you hurt those people?"

"I wasn't here for them, Colonel. I've been watching you for a week or so. I know where you live. I seen that little girl you take to school. Grace, right?"

"Shut the fuck up."

"Cute little thing. Now your wife, Claire, she's got a rockin' body. I can see why you like her. Hell, after this is all over, maybe I'll go visit her."

Nic smiled. He wasn't very good at goading her; it'd take a hell of a lot more than that for her to crack. Him on the other hand, seemed ripe for the picking.

"What did your daddy say when you told him you were getting kicked out of the Corps, Moffett? Is he gonna make you marry your cousin now?"

"What? Fuck you."

"As tempting as that offer is…Heck, who am I kiddin? If I was blind, deaf, and dying tomorrow and the only way I could live was to screw you, I'd pick death." Nic and Moffett mirrored each other's movements as they walked in a circle. "Private Moffett."

"Lance Corporal Moffett."

"As of yesterday, you aren't anything, Mr. Moffett. You have been relieved of duty and officially discharged out of the Corps. You are a disgrace to the uniform you wore, Moffett."

He smiled at her over the sight of the Beretta. "Today is a good day to die, isn't it, Colonel?"

"Is that why you came by, to give me a good-bye hug? Before you have to drive back to Alabama and get your ass whupped by your daddy?"

Nic knew she was laying it on thick, but she'd had enough of being victimized by an asshole like him. He'd stalked her, watched her family. He knew the names of her child and her wife. What else did he know? Why hadn't the Corps put him in the brig instead of just giving him a general discharge?

"You look tired, Colonel." He flashed her a sickly smile. "Maybe you should sit down."

"I'm good. You know that the police will be here any minute."

"Well, I can tell you one of us isn't walking out of here."

"Ah, suicide by cop. How creative of you."

"I'm not dying today, Colonel. While I have nothing to lose, I like breathing. Besides, I like three hots and a cot. I hear Leavenworth isn't so bad. At least that's what Staff Sergeant Jerome said before I helped him on his way to meet god. We prayed together. He told me it was okay, that he was ready to go. Can you believe that?"

Christ. This bastard was evil.

She was the one with everything to lose. If he'd already killed Jerome, then she was just collateral for his case of crazy that he'd stand on when he went to trial.

"Staff Sergeant Jerome didn't do anything to you."

"He knew my secret."

Nic wasn't interested in diving into this scumbag's secrets, but didn't all platoon sergeants know everyone's secrets? They were like your mother who knew everything before you even thought about doing something. At least that's what her crew told her. Want to know what's going in the unit? Talk to the platoon sergeant.

"Whatever he knew, he wasn't telling. He didn't deserve whatever you did to him." Nic's arm was getting tired, so she kept the barrel pointed at Moffett but lowered her arms into a more comfortable position. Her head was pounding and her vision was starting to tunnel again.

"Well, what's done is done." He sat down in a chair and settled in, the Beretta trained on Nic. He pulled out a cigarette and flicked it up into his mouth, one of those bar tricks men did because they thought it impressed women.

"I don't think you're allowed to smoke in here," Nic said, knowing it was pointless but amusing nevertheless.

The music above them stopped. Not a good sign.

Someone was pounding on the door, sounding like they were ready to take it off by its hinges.

"Nic, are you okay?"

❧❧❧❧

Cece stopped Rod as he came off the elevator. "Rod, right? What's going on down there?"

Rod rolled to a stop and looked a little sheepish when he realized that Cece might have been the one to roll on his suicide attempt. She waved him off when he looked like he wanted to speak. It wasn't time to be embarrassed about the way they'd met. She just needed information.

"Nic is down there with some guy named Moffett.

He's got a handgun and Nic took his shotgun away and they are pointing them at each other."

"Shit. Do you know if there are any other ways into that room?"

"There's only the one way."

"Okay, thanks. Claire is probably going to rush you when you get outside, so be prepared. Don't freak her out."

"I'll try not to."

Pushing the Down button, she yelled back at him, "And don't leave. They'll need to take a statement."

"Okay."

Cece pulled her weapon and held it close to her chest. She was amped in a way she hadn't felt since Afghanistan. As the elevator door squished open, she peaked around the door.

Clear.

Moving slowly, she worked her way down the hallway, looking inside each room until she came to the room with the sign. *Group in session, do not disturb.* She didn't have time for this shit.

Pounding on the door, she yelled. "Nic are you, all right?"

Bang.

❧❧❧❧

Nic didn't take her eyes off Moffett as he jerked toward the door and fired a round at the pounding. Without thinking, she fired a shot at him and then stepped to her right and moved in on him as he hit the ground.

"Fucking bitch," he said, blood soaking his pant leg.

She used the muzzle of the shotgun to push the handgun out of his reach.

"You're lucky I didn't blow your fucking head off, asshole."

"Fuck you. We aren't done here."

Nic wanted to laugh but felt like her legs were going to buckle at any minute, so she kicked the gun farther away and pulled up a chair, the shotgun still pointed at the little bastard.

"Oh, we are so done here. You thought just getting tossed from the Marines was your worst offense. You just took a shot at a cop."

"Nic, are you okay?" Cece's voice penetrated through the ringing in her ears.

"It's clear, Cece."

The door eased open an inch or so and then flung wide with Cece rushing in, her gun trained on Moffett. "Is he dead?"

"Nope, but he's going to wish he was if he keeps shooting his mouth off. Pun intended."

Cece keyed her mic and requested medical assistance.

"You okay?"

"Yep. Did everyone get out okay?"

"Yeah, they're all outside." She pushed Moffett over onto his stomach and cuffed him. "I should probably warn you, Claire's outside."

"Oh, shit."

"Sorry, buddy. I needed to confirm this asshole's name and I couldn't remember after we talked about it last week."

Nic took a deep breath and suddenly felt like she'd been pulled through a keyhole without her consent. She buried her face in her hands and tried to get her body to calm down. Adrenaline was a drug like any other, and while she'd gotten used to it when she was overseas, now she felt like a junkie that had just had her first fix in years. Standing, she tried to shake it off. Nic recognized the signs of her PTSD trying to grab purchase in her mind.

"Hey, it's okay. You're safe." Cece roughly rubbed Nic's shoulder and offered a smile.

Nic paced in a small circle around Moffett. She wanted to stomp his ass, beat him to a pulp, and it was taking every ounce of self-control not to. She rubbed her hands up and down her jeans as if the gesture would wipe the incident from her soul.

"Yep, we're clear," Cece said to her mic. "Roger."

The sound of gurneys rushing down the hallway followed by the thud of boots made Nic turn. Behind rescue was Claire and Rod.

"Nic! Nic are you all right?" Claire practically jumped into Nic's arms. "I was so worried. What the fuck happened? Who is this asshole? Did you shoot him?"

Nic raised her eyebrows at Claire and smiled. "I'm fine. We can talk about this later. I'm sure PD has a lot of questions for me." She kissed Claire long and deeply. "I didn't mean to make you worry," she whispered.

"I thought I had lost you again. I can't believe this is happening here, honey."

"Domestic terrorism at its best." Nic looked over at Rod. "You okay, buddy?"

"What a way to welcome me back to group, Nic." Rod forced air through his pursed lips.

"Yeah, sorry. How is everyone else doing?" Nic knew that this would be a big-time trigger for most of them in group.

"I think they'll be okay. They're all outside waiting to find out if you're okay."

Nic fist-bumped Rod and shrugged. "I think I'll be fine."

Moffett was lifted onto his feet. His leg didn't seem to be the worse for wear, lucky for him. Moffett tried to lunge at Nic as she stepped toward him. Cece pushed him backward, practically putting him back on his ass.

"Calm down there, asshole. Aren't you in enough trouble?" Cece watched as they strapped him to the gurney. "So, this is the guy you had the altercation with at the shopette? Not surprised."

"Not the Corps's finest example of a soldier." Nic shook her head.

"Fuck you, Army dyke."

Cece looked at Nic. "Is he talking to me, or you?"

"I'm not Army, so he must be talking to you." Nic laughed as she grabbed Claire's hand and pulled her toward the door.

"I'm talking to you, bitch," Moffett yelled at her back.

Claire stopped, pulled her hand from Nic's, and ran back to Moffett. "I don't know who the heck you are, but you better be glad that you're cuffed. Otherwise, I'd kick the stuffing out of you. You should be ashamed of yourself. Do you kiss your mother with that mouth?"

"Fuck you."

Then Claire did something Nic had never seen her do before: she slapped him so hard across the face a welt instantly appeared. Both Cece and Nic grabbed her and pulled her away at the same time.

"Honey, you can't go around slapping people," Nic said.

"Are you kidding me? You're standing up for him, are you? He tried to kill you, Nic."

"Sweetheart." Nic grabbed Claire's hands and put them at her side, holding her still. "That's assault."

"And I'm going to press charges, too." Moffett squirmed under the restraints.

"Shut up, or I'm going to add more to that little handprint on your face. Are you saying I didn't hit him hard enough?"

Nic needed to diffuse Claire or the impending explosion was going to leave bodies in its wake.

"No, I'm telling him to shut up, and I'm telling you that you don't want to be charged with assault." Nic looked over at Cece, pleading for help.

"Claire, he's going to jail. He took hostages, he has weapons, and if I have anything to say about it, he'll be charged as a domestic terrorist. I'm sure that everyone in the room will tell us that he flat-out threatened Nic's life. So, you don't have to worry. He's going to be going away for a long, long time."

Claire buried her face into Nic's shoulder and started to sob. "I'm sorry. I've never been so close to losing you, Nic. I mean, it's different when it's happening almost right in front of you. I don't know what I would do if he...if he..."

"I know, sweetheart. I know." Nic held her tight as Claire's words hit home. The bombing in Afghanistan had been a detached event. This was personal and right in her face. She hadn't had time to think about anything, let alone her own life. Now it was all starting to sink in, and she suddenly felt like she was going to melt down right in front of Claire. Steeling herself, she held her breath and thought about pulling a box out of a closet and stuffing it with everything that had just happened. She'd deal with it all later. Right now she needed to be strong for Claire, and she'd be damned if she was going to let this asshole have the satisfaction of an implosion.

"Cece, can I take Claire out of here?"

"Sure. Why don't you wait for me outside? Rod, do you have a few minutes to tell me what happened?"

"Sure."

Nic fist-bumped Rod again. "Thanks, buddy."

"No problem. See you outside."

Nic wrapped her arm around Claire's shoulder and walked her to the elevator. How could the world be so screwed up? She was in just as much danger at home as she was out in the field.

Now what?

Epilogue

Two months later

The church hummed as everyone mingled before taking their seats. Nic recognized a few faces, but most were foreign to her. She had come a long way since the shooting. While she still hated going to group, she felt as if she owed it to them to stay on and work through the issues that had risen out of the events with Moffett. The court case against Moffett was moving at a snail's pace. The Marine Corps had first dibs on the man, and Monterey wanted him in their court system as well, so the fight had begun over who had jurisdiction. However, that was for another day. Today was a day for weddings, happiness, and thoughts of the future.

Nic smiled over at Claire, who looked stunning in her dress. She never wanted to lose this feeling of joy each time she saw Claire. Her heart raced and she couldn't wait to get her home and love her. While time and a few wrinkles might change her outward appearance, her heart would never wane. Nic could feel herself tear up as she bit her lip.

Claire waved at Nic and winked. She made a motion at her throat, like she was straightening Nic's tie.

Yep, she would never lose that tingle. Nic pulled at the bow tie around her neck and tried to straighten it. She pointed to it as she looked at Claire, who gave her a thumbs-up.

"You ready, Colonel?" Rod rolled closer to Nic and raised his fist for the bump.

"The bigger question is, are you ready?" Nic hit her fist against his and smiled. "This is a big step, buddy."

"I think we're beyond big steps. I mean Melody is in her last trimester and I don't want my kid coming into this world without a legal dad."

"I don't think legality has anything to do with it, Rod. You're going to be an amazing father." Nic grabbed his shoulder and squeezed. "I'd want you for a dad," she said, hoping it reassured the young man.

"Thanks."

Rod's mom was his only family member in attendance today, and according to Rod it was better than nothing. He never talked about his father, and they both agreed that it took more than biology to make a dad. It took love, commitment, and heart, and Rod had all of that in droves. Yep, baby Rod was a lucky kid.

The minister stepped between them. "Are we ready?"

"I think so," Rod said, turning his wheelchair around to look down the aisle. The music started, and on cue Melody walked through the arch of the church. Nic looked over at Claire who was staring back at her, tears filling her eyes as she blew Nic a kiss. Nic blew one back and rubbed at her eyes.

Yep. Rod wasn't the only lucky person in that church to find their soulmate.

If you liked this book?

Reviews help an author's books get discovered and if you have enjoyed this book, please do the author the honor of posting a review on Goodreads, Amazon, Barnes & Noble or anywhere you purchased the book. Or perhaps share a posting on your social media sites to help spread the word to your friends.

About the Author

Isabella lives on the central coast with her wife, and three sons. She teaches college and in her spare time, which there seems to be little of lately, she is working on her writers retreat in the Sierra foothills. She is a GLCS award winner for Always Faithful and a finalist for Scarlet Masquerade. She also finaled in the International National Book awards and has two honorable mentions in the Rainbow Awards.

She also writes under the nom de plume - Jett Abbott. A darker, rogue who's a motorcycle enthusiast and loves people watching.

Like her fan page for the latest in news on readings, appearances and books.

https://www.facebook.com/isabella.sapphirebooks

or

www.sapphirebooks.com/isabella.html

Check out Isabella's other books

Award winning novel - *Always Faithful* - ISBN - 978-0-982860-80-9

Major Nichol "Nic" Caldwell is the only survivor of her helicopter crash in Iraq. She is left alone to wonder why she and she alone survived. Survivor's guilt has nothing on the young Major as she is forced to deal with the scars, both physical and mental, left from her ordeal overseas. Before the accident, she couldn't think of doing anything else in her life.

Claire Monroe is your average military wife, with a loving husband and a little girl. She is used to the time apart from her husband. In fact, it was one of the reasons she married him. Then, one day, her life is turned upside down when she gets a visit from the Marine Corps.

Can these two women come to terms with the past and finally find happiness, or will their shared sense of honor keep them apart?

Forever Faithful - ISBN – 978-1-939062-75-8

Life is what happens when you make other plans, and Nic and Claire have just found out that life and the Marine Corps have other plans for their lives. Nic Caldwell has served her country, met the woman of her dreams, and has reached the rank of Lieutenant Colonel. She's studying at one of the nation's most prestigious military universities, setting her sights on a research position after graduation. Things couldn't be better and then it happens; a sudden assignment to Afghanistan derails any thoughts of marriage and wedded bliss. Another combat zone, another tragedy, and Nic suddenly finds herself fighting for her life. Claire Monroe loves her new life in Monterey. She's finally where she wants to be, getting ready to start her master's program at the local university, watching her daughter, Grace, growing up, and getting ready to marry the love of her life. What could possibly derail a perfect life? The Marine Corps. Will Nic survive Afghanistan? Can Claire step up and be the strength in their relationship? Or will this overseas assignment and a catastrophic accident divide their once happy home?

American Yakuza - ISBN - 978-0-9828608-3-0

Luce Potter straddles three cultures as she strives to live with the ideals of family, honor, and duty. When her grandfather passes the family business to her, Luce finds out that power, responsibility and justice come with a price. Is it a price she's willing to die for?

Brooke Erickson lives the fast-paced life of an investigative journalist living on the edge until it all comes crashing down around her one night in Europe. Stateside, Brooke learns to deal with a new reality when she goes to work at a financial magazine and finds out things aren't always as they seem.

Can two women find enough common ground for love or will their two different worlds and cultures keep them apart?

American Yakuza II - The Lies that Bind - ISBN - 978-10939062-20-8

Luce Potter runs her life and her business with an iron fist and complete control until lies and deception unravel her world. The shadow of betrayal consumes Luce, threatening to destroy the most precious thing in her life, Brooke Erickson.

Brooke Erickson finds herself on the outside of Luce's life looking in. As events spiral out of control Brooke can only watch as the woman she loves pushes her further away. Suddenly, devastated and alone, Brooke refuses to let go without an explanation.

Colby Water, a federal agent investigating the ever-elusive Luce Potter, discovers someone from her past is front and center in her investigation of the Yakuza crime leader. Before she can put the crime boss in prison, she must confront the ultimate deception in her professional life.

When worlds collide, betrayal, dishonor and death are inevitable. Can Luce and Brooke survive the explosion?

America Yakuza III- Razor's Edge - ISBN - 978-1-943353-81-1

Luce Potter lives by a code of honor. Push her and she shoves back, harder. There's only one problem: Luce has just found out that revenge is a knife that cuts both ways. Now that her lover Brooke has survived the attack on her life, Luce has only one thing on her mind, and his name is Frank. Unfortunately, someone walks into her life that she didn't see coming. Brooke Erickson has survived an attack so brutal it's left a permanent scar on her soul. All she wants to do now is go home and finish recuperating with her lover, Luce Potter, by her side. An unexpected event puts Brooke at the head of the Yakuza family. Can she command the respect necessary to lead it through the crisis? Luce and Brooke's worlds are upending. Can each do what's necessary to survive and return to a new normal

Executive Disclosure- ISBN - 978-0-9828608-3-0

When a life is threatened, it takes a special breed of person to step in front of a bullet. Chad Morgan's job has put her life on the line more times that she can count. Getting close to the client is expected; getting too close could be deadly for Chad. Reagan Reynolds wants the top job at Reynolds Holdings and knows how to play the game like "the boys." She's not above using her beauty and body as currency to get what she wants. Shocked to find out someone wants her dead, Reagan isn't thrilled at the prospect of needing protection as she tries to convince the board she's the right woman for a man's job. How far will a killer go to get what they want? Secrets and deception twist the rules of the game as a killer closes in. How far will Chad go to protect her beautiful, but challenging client?

Surviving Reagan - ISBN - 978-1-939062-38-3

Chad Caldwell has finally worked through the betrayal of her former client and lover, Reagan Reynolds. Putting the pieces of her life back in order, she finds herself on a collision course with that past when she takes on a new client, the future first lady. Unfortunately, Chad's newest job puts her in the cross-hairs of a domestic terrorist determined to release a virus that could kill thousands of women. Reagan Reynolds has paid for her sins and is ready to start a new life. Attending a business conference in Abu Dhabi gives her the opportunity to prove to her father and herself that she's worthy of a fresh start. Her past will intersect with her future at the conference when she accidentally comes face-to-face with Chad Caldwell. Time is running out. Will Reagan confront Chad? Can she convince Chad she's changed, or will death part them forever?

Broken Shield - ISBN - 978-0-982860-82-3

Tyler Jackson, former paramedic now firefighter, has seen her share of death up close. The death of her wife caused Tyler to rethink her career choices, but the death of her mother two weeks later cemented her return to the ranks of firefighter. Her path of self-destruction and womanizing is just a front to hide the heartbreak and devastation she lives with every day. Tyler's given up on finding love and having the family she's always wanted. When tragedy strikes her life for a second time she finds something she thought she lost.

Ashley Henderson loves her job. Ignoring her mother's advice, she opts for a career in law enforcement. But, Ashley hides a secret that soon turns her life upside down. Shame, guilt and fear keep Ashley from venturing forward and finding the love she so desperately craves. Her life comes crashing down around her in one swift moment forcing her to come clean about her secrets and her life.

Can two women thrust together by one traumatic event survive and find love together, or will their past force them apart?

Scarlet Assassin - ISBN - 978-1-939062-36-9

Selene Hightower is a killer for hire. A vampire who walks in both the light and the darkness, but lately darkness has a stronger pull. Her unfinished business could cost her the ability to live in the light, throwing her permanently back into the black ink of evil.

Doctor Francesca Swartz led a boring life filled with test tubes, blood trials, and work. One exploratory night, in a world of leather and torture, she is intrigued by a dark and solitary soul. She surrenders to temptation and the desire to experience something new, only to discover that it might alter her life forever.

Will Selene allow the light to win over the darkness threatening the edges of her life? Two women wonder if they can co-exist despite vast differences, as worlds collide and threaten to destroy any hope of happiness. Who will win?

The Gate - ISBN – 978-1-943353-93-4

Valhalla is for warriors that die in battle. What of those who don't have a hero's death? Where do they go? The inter-world is in chaos and has become the heart of the battleground in the war between Paladins and Gatekeepers. Harley doesn't know it yet, but she's at ground zero. A night of drinking, to forget a cheating girlfriend, is about to change her life forever. A birthmark—or a birthright—sets her on a direct path to a woman who claims to have known her for centuries. Not ready to accept her Paladin mantel, she needs proof—and that proof is out to destroy her. A protector by birth, Dawn was bred to preserve the delicate cycle of life and death. Protecting a Paladin is to be mated for eternity, usually without the sex, but Harley's allure is universally compelling. Harley's rise in status to The Chosen complicates things further as Dawn finds herself fighting for her own heart, as well as battling her biggest nemesis and brother, Lucius. Lucius, lord of the Gatekeepers, is out to kill souls moving to their next life. He wants Harley in his corner and he isn't about to let a little sibling rivalry stand in the way, no matter what it takes. Harley find herself caught up in Lucius's tempting promise of power, but cannot shake the soul-tugging love she feels with Dawn. Will Dawn convince Harley in time to embrace her Paladin destiny and save the souls looking for their gate, or will Lucius be able to sway Harley to throw in with the Gatekeepers?

Twisted Deception - ISBN - 978-1-939062-47-5

There are two types of people who can't look you in the eyes: someone trying to hide a lie and someone trying to hide their love.

Addie Blake's life isn't black and white--more like a series of short bursts of color that sustain her until the next eruption. She isn't a ladder-climber in the corporate world. Instead, she works long hours at the office and even at home, something her mechanic girlfriend, Drake Hogan, can't stand. If Addie can't focus on Drake, then Drake finds arm candy that will. After a long week of late nights and a series of text-messaged demands, each one a bigger bomb than the last, Addie has had enough of her Motor Girl.

Greyson Hollister inhabits a world where everything is either black and white, or money green. She's a polished, certified workaholic. As head of Integrated Financial, she has built the ladder others want to climb. Now she intends to attend a business mixer to confront a rumormonger and kill merger rumors involving her company.

Detective Nancy Hill, the lead detective on the Elevator Rapist task force, has just been called in to investigate an attack at Integrated Financial. She can't quite put her finger on it, but something doesn't add up with this latest assault, and Greyson Hollister isn't exactly lending a helping hand.

A storm's brewing on the horizon. Can Addie and Greyson weather it, or will it blow them over?

Writing as Jett Abbott

Scarlet Masquerade - ISBN - 978-0-982860-81-6

What do you say to the woman you thought died over a century ago? Will time heal all wounds or does it just allow them to fester and grow? A.J. Locke has lived over two centuries and works like a demon, both figuratively and literally. As the owner of a successful pharmaceutical company that specializes in blood research, she has changed the way she can live her life. Wanting for nothing, she has smartly compartmentalized her life so that when she needs to, she can pick up and start all over again, which happens every twenty years or so. Love is not an emotion A.J. spends much time on. Since losing the love of her life to the plague one hundred fifty years ago, she vowed to never travel down that road again. That isn't to say she doesn't have women when she wants them, she just wants them on her terms and that doesn't involve a long term commitment.

A.J.'s cool veneer is peeled back when she sees the love of her life in a lesbian bar, in the same town, in the same day and time in which she lives. Is her mind playing tricks on her? If not, how did Clarissa survive the plague when she had made A.J. promise never to change her?

Clarissa Graham is a university professor who has lived an obscure life teaching English literature. She has made it a point to stay off the radar and never become involved with anything that resembles her past life. Every once in a while Clarissa has an itch that needs to be scratched, so she finds an out of the way location to scratch it. She keeps her personal life separate from her professional one, and in doing so she is able to keep her secrets to herself. Suddenly, her life is turned upside down when someone tries to kill her. She finds herself in the middle of an assassination plot with no idea who wants her dead.

Isabella